The Christmas Project
Stories From Hartford

Amanda Hamm

ISBN: 978-0-9850659-8-0

The Christmas Project is a work of fiction. All names, characters, places, events, etc. are products of the author's imagination or are used fictitiously.

Chapter 1

The coin counter used to be the most annoying sound at the bank. In recent weeks, however, Gaby Bryant was starting to rank the sound of her own name in the top spot on that list. She had a relatively new coworker who insisted on calling her Gabrielle – even though no one else did – and she called her Gabrielle every single chance she got. They were both tellers. Every time there was a break in customers or a moment when neither was counting money, Krista would say, "Gabrielle, have I told you…" or "Gabrielle, guess what happened when…" or "Gabrielle, you'll never believe…" She would keep talking until one of them had to focus on work.

Gaby had enjoyed the quiet when Krista took a few days off before Thanksgiving. Now it was the day after and she was back. She leaned towards Gaby as soon as her customer's back was turned. "Gabrielle," she said, "did you see him?"

"Did I see who?"

"The new guy."

"The new loan officer? I thought he wasn't starting until Monday?"

"Me, too. But he's definitely here. I saw him talking to Bob when I went back to use the bathroom. And get this… no wedding ring." Krista nodded significantly.

"That doesn't mean he isn't seeing someone."

"True. You should ask him."

Gaby shook her head. "Why don't you ask him since you're the one who cares?"

"You'll care when you see him. Someone needs to go out with him and you know I can't because of Kevin." Krista rolled her eyes when she said this. Kevin was her boyfriend. She always talked about him as though he was a burden. Gaby tried to tune out whenever Krista talked about her love life. Krista was thirty-one and had already been married and divorced twice… to the same man. Not Kevin.

"You know what he did now, Gabrielle?"

Gaby shook her head.

"That man!" Krista exclaimed. "He gave all our turkey leftovers to his mom without asking me first. And then he expected me to be happy that she was going to make us a pot pie out of them."

Gaby tried to pretend she was listening as Krista went on about what else happened at her Thanksgiving party and the other ways that Kevin had ruined it. The topic continued most of the day. It was interrupted by customers and other work-related tasks. But every lull was filled with further descriptions of Krista's Thanksgiving. She did not at any point mention gratitude.

Just before the end of the day, when both of them were helping customers, Krista said, "Gabrielle." She didn't say anything else, but when Gaby looked at her, she moved her eyes briefly towards the front door.

Gaby glanced past her customer and saw Bob Chapman, the president of the Hartford Bank, standing next to a man she didn't recognize.

Hartford was a small town, small enough that it was unusual for Gaby to have a customer she couldn't greet by name. Even without Krista's hint, she would have guessed this was the new employee. He had short dark hair and a close-cropped beard. His suit fit well and Gaby felt a slight flash of warmth as he also glanced in her direction.

She quickly refocused on her duties. There were only a few more people to help before the front door would be locked and the tellers could finish for the day.

"Gabrielle, do you remember when I had my hair done last week? Kevin didn't even notice."

"Hmm…" Gaby nodded slightly, but she was trying to look as though she needed to concentrate. Krista had changed her hair by dying it one shade lighter. It was already so white-blonde that Gaby hadn't noticed it either until Krista said something.

"I thought it was good to get it done before all the holiday parties, but now I'm wondering if I did it too early. I'm going to have to touch it up again before Christmas."

"Okay," Gaby said without looking up.

"Gabrielle?"

"What?"

"Gabrielle?" Krista repeated.

"I said… oh!" Gaby lifted her head and saw that the new guy was standing in front of her station.

"Hi," he said with a smile that showed off his straight white teeth.

"Hello," Gaby said, "you must be new here."

He held out a hand to her. "I'm Jared Greener. You're Gabrielle?"

"Gaby," she said as she gave his hand a quick shake. "Gaby Bryant. It's nice to meet you."

Jared looked expectantly at Krista.

"I'm Krista Farrington."

Jared nodded. "And how long have you ladies worked here?"

"I've only been here four months," Krista said. "Gabrielle's been here forever."

"Really?" Jared gave Gaby a look of amused disbelief. "I'm sorry but you don't look old enough to have been here anywhere near forever."

Gaby shrugged. "It's been about three and a half years." She guessed by the apparently long string of previous jobs that Krista had mentioned that three and a half years might sound like forever to her for someone to be at the same job.

Jared smiled from one woman to the other for a moment. His gaze lingered on Gaby as he said, "Well, I'm sure we'll all enjoy working together. I'll let you finish up for tonight."

He was barely out of earshot before Krista started again. "Gabrielle, he is totally going to ask you out. You have to tell me all about it. Maybe you two can go to the office party together."

"I think I'm done here. I'll see you Monday, Krista." Gaby grabbed her things and headed towards the back as she waved. She avoided discussing anything personal with Krista whenever possible. But she would have been in a hurry to get home anyway. It was finally time to decorate.

Gaby's family had always decorated for Christmas the day after Thanksgiving. It was convenient when she and her sisters had the day off school. She had been worried that it wouldn't be as exciting to decorate a place by herself, especially after a full day at work. Owen had been making it fun though.

Gaby lived in a very symmetrical white building with four apartments, two on the first floor and two on the second. Gaby's apartment was upstairs on the left and Owen's was on the right. He was her best friend. The sooner she got her side decked out the sooner she could start giving him a hard time about his dreary, non-festive side.

The bank's dress code was rather formal. Gaby left her red blouse on because it was a Christmas color, but she traded her black skirt and heels for jeans and sneakers. She had pulled her decorations out of the closet the previous weekend to see if the lights still worked. Only one of her strings had died so she didn't bother buying more. Her artificial tree was only three feet tall so she'd use most of her lights outside. She dragged her end table next to the window by the front door and put the tree on top where it would be seen through the window.

The ornaments could wait. She put on her coat and gloves and took the rest of the lights outside. She put the first string around the door and two around the bottom of the black metal railing. She was wrapping the last string around the top of the railing when Owen appeared on the stairs.

"Already?" he said.

She stopped what she was doing to face him. "Don't pretend to be surprised. You know this is official Put Up Your Pretty Christmas Decorations or Your Next-Door-Neighbor Will Start Calling You a Grinch Day."

Owen smiled. "Is that what they're calling it now?"

"That's what I'm calling it. You *are* going to do at least some decorating this year, aren't you?"

"I really don't see the point."

"Where is your Christmas spirit?"

"I think maybe you have enough for both of us."

Gaby shook her head. "That didn't fly last year either. I'm not saying you have to go nuts. But you could at least get a tree."

"A tree? That takes more work than most everything else."

"But it's fun work," Gaby insisted.

"No such thing." He held up the plastic bag he was carrying. "I stopped at the Market on the way home because I felt like cooking. Want to join me?"

"Sure. How long?"

4

"It's just spaghetti. Maybe twenty minutes."

"Perfect. That'll give me just enough time to finish up."

"All right. See you soon." Owen pulled his keys from his pocket and went into his side of the top floor.

Gaby went back to wrapping her lights. She put a few ornaments on her tree and tied her stocking to her bedroom door handle. There was no mantle or fireplace in her tiny apartment. She left her coat behind when she dashed over to knock on Owen's door, an action that had become very familiar over the last few years.

Gaby and Owen had actually known each other most of their lives. They graduated in the same class and Hartford High School was small enough that everyone knew everyone at least by sight, but the two of them hadn't spent enough time together to like or dislike each other. They went to different colleges and both came back to Hartford when they finished. Gaby had only been in her apartment for a week when she noticed Owen moving in next door. They chatted briefly about the four years they'd been away and then went about their own business.

They might have simply continued as acquaintances if it hadn't been for the spider. The week after Owen moved in, on a Saturday morning, Gaby had been sitting in her apartment watching TV when she felt the need for a drink of water. She went into the kitchen – which was practically the same room in the limited space – and grabbed a glass from her cupboard. She turned around and froze in fear.

There on the lower cabinet, blocking her path to the sink, was a hairy spider the size of a small dog. Or at least that was how big it seemed to Gaby. Without thinking, she ran outside to knock on Owen's door. Her panic was a lot stronger than her embarrassment as she begged him to please, please come over and take care of the intruder.

He captured the pest and took it outside without either of them saying much else. It was a bit awkward as they were both in their jammies. The next day she baked cookies and brought him some as a proper thank you. It turned out that he liked cookies as much as she disliked spiders. They exchanged phone numbers and immediately began talking and visiting regularly. Three and a half years later, Gaby was *almost* grateful for the spider as Owen opened his door for her.

"Five minutes from being ready," he said.

She came in quickly so they could close the door against the chill and then she said, "Good. We'll have time to decorate." Gaby held up her hands. She had a glittery silver ball ornament in each one. "Where should I put these?"

"On *your* tree."

"My tree is already beautiful. Your place on the other hand…" Gaby looked around. Owen's apartment was actually nicer than hers. He had newer furniture and he kept it very clean. She always had piles of some sort of project sitting around. But there was not a single item in sight to indicate that Christmas was approaching. "I know," she said, "I'll put them on this plant you haven't killed yet."

She walked towards the spikey plant near a dark brown sofa. Owen's mom had given him the plant in the summer. He had been insisting for months that he wasn't going to be able to keep it alive. Gaby hooked the ornaments between the leaves and smiled.

Owen shrugged and turned to the kitchen. Gaby followed and watched as he dumped the noodles into a waiting strainer and back into the pan. The table was already set. Gaby sat facing the counter, which was her usual side, while Owen took some garlic bread from the oven.

"That smells good," she said.

Owen nodded in agreement and put it on the table. He sat across from her and said a quick prayer and then sliced a few pieces of bread.

"So how was work?" Gaby asked.

"The usual."

"Do you regret not taking the day off?"

"So I could stay home and put up a Christmas tree?" He was smirking at her and she refused to take the bait.

"Lots of things you could have done with the long weekend."

"How was your day?" he asked. "Krista was back, right?"

"Yeah, so not exactly a quiet day. They hired someone to replace Nancy and I met him today."

"What's he like?"

"I'm not sure," Gaby said. "I really didn't talk to him for more than thirty seconds but… he's younger and better looking than I expected."

6

"Oh?" Owen pushed his eyebrows up. "So you're saying you're interested in finding out more about him?"

"Maybe. He kind of looked at me like... sort of like he wouldn't mind talking to *me* more."

"I'm not surprised that he's interested, but would that be a problem?"

"What do you mean?"

"Does the bank have a policy against, you know, fraternizing?"

"Only when there's a direct supervisor involved so it wouldn't be an issue." Gaby fought off a slightly uncomfortable feeling. It felt as though there was something wrong with the conversation but she couldn't identify the problem. "But like I said, I just met the guy. If he turns out to be unavailable or unappealing... you're going to pretend I never mentioned him, right?"

"I can do that."

Gaby focused on a few bites of her dinner. The sauce was from a jar and it wasn't that difficult to boil noodles, but she still appreciated his effort. If it wasn't for Owen, more of her meals would start frozen. "Thanks for cooking," she said. "And what you said a minute ago about not being surprised a guy was interested?"

"Yeah?"

"I'm going to take that as a compliment so thanks for that, too."

"You're welcome."

"Are you going to thank me now?"

Owen squinted around his light blue eyes in an expression somewhere between confused and amused. "Why am I thanking you?"

"For the ornaments."

His eyes settled on amused. "Oh, am I thanking you for the useless decorations or for helping me kill the plant?"

"How are two tiny ornaments going to kill the plant?"

"That much glitter can't be good for anything. I think it's going to go blind first."

"Your plant can see?"

"Don't sound so skeptical. It can hear you, too."

Gaby burst into laughter. "You are ridiculous," she said.

"*I'm* ridiculous. I'm not the one who spends all of December covering everything with red and green. And glitter."

"That's called holiday cheer. I sprinkle things with holiday cheer."

"Just don't sprinkle any more of it in my apartment."

Gaby smiled. "Does this mean you don't want any cookies this year?"

Owen looked defeated. He sighed dramatically. "I guess if the price of Christmas cookies is some..." he paused to make air quotes "...holiday cheer, then you can sign me up for a tiny bit."

"Awesome." Gaby rubbed her hands together. "I'm bringing something good next time."

"But I want extra sprinkles on my cookies."

"If you help me make them, you can put on as many sprinkles as you want."

"We'll see."

Gaby had tried to talk Owen into helping with the cookies the last few years with no luck. She didn't intend to give up unless she got a firm no. And there was always next year.

She helped him clean up after dinner and then they sat on the sofa. Owen's TV was nearly twice the size of Gaby's. He pulled up the list of recorded shows for her to choose one. When they spent an evening at her place, Owen got to choose from her list. There was enough overlap in their tastes for the system to work most of the time.

Halfway through the show, they heard a siren in the distance. Gaby jumped up and said, "It's time! Where are your shoes?" She was walking over to the front door to retrieve his shoes before she finished talking.

Owen pushed the pause button. "Are you really going to make me go outside?" he asked.

She put the shoes on the floor in front of him. "Hurry up. We don't want to miss him."

She watched the top of his blonde head as he slipped his feet into his shoes and worked on the laces. The siren was getting louder. She grabbed his hand and tried to pull him up even though he outweighed her by about fifty pounds. "Come on," she said.

He smiled slightly at her enthusiasm and let her drag him outside. They continued to hear the siren for a minute and a family across the street appeared on their porch as well. "You know they

8

go up and down all the streets so we didn't need to hurry," he said.

"This way we're ready," Gaby said. She was rubbing her hands together as neither of them had put on a coat.

Owen grabbed one of her dark brown curls and pulled it straight before letting it spring back. "I notice you've been wearing your hair down a lot more often lately."

"Yeah, it's *finally* getting long enough." Gaby had nearly waist-length hair through college and up until the summer before last. She went in for a trim and saw a sign for Locks of Love. She impulsively decided that shoulder-length hair would be a nice change for a good cause. But she had underestimated her natural curls. Without the extra weight, they coiled up into a rather triangle-shaped nightmare. She shed more than a few tears over the result. She had expected Owen to make fun of her for crying over hair. He hugged her instead. Sometimes he was very nice to have around. Her hair now landed just past her shoulders even when it was in full curl.

Owen watched those curls bounce as Gaby hopped up and down to keep warm. "Let me get a jacket for you," he said with his hand on the knob.

"No! He's coming." She pointed to the corner where a fire truck was turning onto their street. A second one was right behind it. Both trucks had lights and sirens going and were covered with strings of Christmas lights. On the back of the second truck was a man in a Santa suit, waving wildly.

Gaby returned the wave and Owen put his hand up for a second. This was a Hartford tradition, the arrival of Santa the day after Thanksgiving on the back of a fire truck. Gaby had waved at Santa every year for as long as she could remember and her favorite parts of Christmas were the things that stayed the same every year.

Owen opened the door as soon as the trucks had passed and ushered Gaby inside. She was rubbing her hands together and he put his on top of hers.

"How are your hands still warm?" she asked.

He shrugged.

"This is great. Now that Santa's officially in town, the letters will start coming in."

"I'm not helping," he said as he continued to gently squeeze her hands.

"I didn't even ask yet."

"I'm still not helping."

"Hey," Gaby said, "do you know who Santa is this year? I heard Mr. Overmeyer couldn't do it."

Owen nodded. "David Schmidt."

"Wait a minute. Isn't he your uncle?"

"Yeah."

"So you had a family member playing Santa and you still weren't going to go outside?"

"Well, because he's family he knows I'm not six." He gave her a fairly cheeky grin and for some reason it made all of Gaby's attention focus on the fact that he was still holding her hands.

She pulled them away and said, "I'm warm enough. Let's finish the show."

Chapter 2

Gaby sat with her parents at church in the same pew they had claimed most Sundays while she was growing up. They watched as the first purple candle was lit. It was the only Advent wreath the church had used in her lifetime, though the pink and purple ribbons had been replaced at least once. She waved at Owen on the other side of the church before she left. He was also sitting with his parents and his brother.

If she didn't know Jimmy was only two years younger, she would not have believed it. Owen more or less looked his twenty-six years. Jimmy still looked about fifteen.

Both young men climbed into the backseat of their parents' car as they left. Saint Christopher Church was in Port Harris. The ride back to Hartford was roughly thirty minutes, depending on who was driving, so it made sense for the family to ride together. Jimmy nudged his brother at one point with a questioning glance and Owen shook his head and let his eyes fall on their parents.

Their mom made waffles for lunch while their dad made a warm fruit topping for them. It was delicious and the four chatted pleasantly. They had just been together for Thanksgiving with a lot of extended family and their conversation involved memories of the day and recapping of news that one or more of them might have missed.

Owen and Jimmy left at the same time. Instead of heading straight around the corner to his apartment, Owen sat on the porch steps and slumped over his knees. Jimmy sighed and sat on the other side of the steps. "This is about Gaby, isn't it?" he asked.

Owen stared at the sidewalk ahead of them. "She met someone."

"She met someone?"

"There's a new guy at the bank and she said... she said she might be interested in him."

"I don't know why you torture yourself, man. You should move."

"I can't move. Besides the whole lease thing, I can't… not if there's even a little chance that things might change between us."

Jimmy shook his head. "You're pathetic."

"I'm pathetic? You're the one who likes to watch the engaged woman run through town."

"Hey, I just appreciate the fact that Rebecca is an attractive woman. I'm not in love with someone who thinks I'm a girl."

Owen reached over and gave Jimmy a shove. "She doesn't think I'm a girl."

"Really? Didn't she once ask you what you were going to wear somewhere?"

"That's because she's a girl, not because she thinks I'm one."

Jimmy shrugged. "Well, if she just met the guy, you may not have anything to worry about anyway."

"It's just that I thought there were a few times lately when there was a spark, you know. But if she doesn't think it's weird to mention another guy then I was clearly wrong."

"You're always wrong. I'd think you'd be used to it by now."

"Very funny," Owen said dryly.

"Well, I don't know how you expect things to change if you don't tell her you want it to change."

"I can't tell her."

"You'd rather continue being pathetic?"

"If she's happy with our relationship the way it is then I don't want to ruin it for her."

"That's kind of mushy. Maybe you are a girl."

Owen shoved his brother again. "Stop saying that."

"Stop hitting me before I have to arrest you for assaulting a police officer." Jimmy was smiling and pretending to nurse his shoulder.

"Just tell me what I'm supposed to do."

"All right, man." Jimmy put on a more serious expression and appeared to give the matter some actual thought. "I guess you need to make her not happy with the relationship."

"What are you talking about?"

"Start acting like a guy."

12

Owen held up his fist like he was going to punch his brother's arm.

"I mean," Jimmy said, "like a guy she'd want to date. You know, make some romantic gestures. But not too obvious because then you might as well tell her."

"So be obvious but not too obvious?" Owen rolled his eyes. "You are so helpful."

Jimmy stood up and stuffed his hands into his jacket pockets. "Don't ask for my advice if you're going to mock it."

Owen stood as well. "I guess it's not as though I have a better idea."

"No, you don't," Jimmy said with a wave. "Later."

The walk home was short, but cold. When he got inside, Owen was still thinking that he didn't have a better idea because there might not be one. Gaby might still view him as a friend no matter what he did or didn't do but perhaps it was time he at least tried to turn things in another direction.

****

"Gabrielle, I bought the cutest pair of shoes yesterday."

Gaby tried not to sigh as she turned to Krista. "Yeah? What color?"

Krista rolled her eyes. "They were $300 shoes marked down to only $70. I was going to buy them no matter what color they were. But they're a beautiful deep purple with braided straps across the toes and four-inch heels. Obviously, I can't wear them here so I don't know when I'll get a chance."

Gaby tried to nod as though she understood the need for shoes that might never be worn. "Did you put up your tree this weekend?" she asked.

"Kevin has one, but I wouldn't let him put it up. I need a real tree and he was too lazy to get one. I'll try to make him do it next weekend. Oh, Gabrielle!" A new thought always made Krista try to get Gaby's attention even if they were already in the middle of a conversation. "I also stopped at the Market and I found out that someone named Martin Filmore has a two-bedroom for rent. Do you know who that is?"

"Yeah. That name doesn't sound familiar to you?"

13

Krista cocked her head to the side. "You forget I've only lived in Hartford for six months. I know you were born knowing everybody else around here, but I haven't had a chance to catch up."

"Still," Gaby said, "Martin Filmore is the mayor."

"Oh." Krista looked thoughtful for a moment. "Actually, that still doesn't help me. Do you know what kind of landlord he'd be?"

Gaby shrugged. "You thinking of moving?"

"Kevin and I can't get a moment away from each other in that tiny little place of his. The lease is up in February and I figured it wouldn't hurt to look around."

"Where is the apartment?"

"It's a house actually. I think Mabel said it was on Washington Street. Oh, good... kids." Krista was looking towards the front door where two young boys, around ten or eleven years old, had walked in. She was watching them suspiciously and sighed noticeably when one of them dropped the can of coins he had been holding.

The flat maroon carpet was surprisingly effective at muffling the noise and the commotion was mostly visual. Coins rolled in several directions away from the boys. The boy who had been carrying the coins dove to the ground to begin scooping them back into the can while his friend began running around him trying to stomp on the moving coins. One of which he chased all the way to the opposite wall.

Gaby came from around the counter to help. She was glad she was wearing her nice black pants because she couldn't squat in a skirt. The boy was thoroughly red-faced and re-dropping almost half the coins in his rush to return them to the can, which had a peanut label on the outside.

"You're one of Mabel's grandsons, right?" she asked, thinking that small talk might distract him from his embarrassment.

He nodded.

"Aiden?" she guessed.

He shook his head and said, "Landon."

"Really? You've gotten big."

Landon made a disgusted noise. "People always say that, but I'm like the shortest kid in my class."

Gaby dumped a handful of coins into his can as the other boy

14

returned with a few stray quarters. He plunked them into the can without saying anything and knelt to grab coins from the largest pile, which was diminishing quickly.

A larger set of hands began working on coins as well and Gaby realized it was her new coworker, Jared Greener. He looked at her playfully and said, "Gaby, you're not supposed to throw the customer's coins on the floor."

Gaby smiled.

"I dropped them," Landon said flatly.

"I think Mr. Greener was trying to be funny."

Landon nodded. He looked as though he understood but still didn't think it was funny.

Jared said, "I guess I tried and failed." He looked at Landon. "I've heard women like a sense of humor. You should try to develop one while you're still young so you'll do better than me."

Landon didn't even nod. He simply stopped trying to hide his puzzled expression.

"I think we got them all," Gaby said as she stood. Both boys stood up, but their eyes didn't leave the carpet. Jared smoothed his tie and smiled at Gaby as he turned away.

"There's one over here," Krista called from behind the counter. She was pointing a few feet in front of her station. Landon's quiet friend jogged over to pick it up. The boys waited until Gaby had resumed her position before handing her the coins to deposit.

Jared returned to the front as they were closing up for the day. He smiled politely at Krista before focusing most of his attention on Gaby. "If those boys had been a few years older, they'd have been about ten times more embarrassed to drop their coins in front of beautiful women."

"I felt so bad for them," Gaby replied. "But at least I think we got all their money."

Jared lowered his head in fake disappointment and looked at Gaby through his dark lashes. "I guess I failed again."

"Failed?"

"First I wasn't funny and now my attempt to compliment you didn't work. What's a guy gotta do?"

"Depends," Gaby said. If he was going to flirt, she could play along.

"On what?"

15

"Depends what said guy is trying to accomplish."

He met her eyes with his. "Just trying to get your attention."

Gaby didn't look away. "This works."

"It's a start," he said with a slow smile. He took a few steps away from her counter before he broke the connection.

"Gabrielle," Krista said, "that was hot. He is totally going to ask you out. I knew you'd care that he was single."

Gaby tried to smile benignly. She had a feeling she was going to enjoy discussing her own love life even less than Krista's. She was likely getting ahead of herself anyway. Perhaps Jared didn't have any real intentions. But what was with that annoying feeling that she wouldn't think that was bad? New single men were somewhat rare in Hartford. Why wasn't she more excited to meet one?

****

It was shortly after 8 pm on Monday when Gaby sent Owen a text that said: I need a break. Want to come over?

Instead of a return message, she received a knock on her door. She opened it and Owen said, "A break from what? Yes."

"My mom gave me more boxes."

"Find anything good?"

"Not exactly but... what are you hiding?" Gaby had noticed that Owen suspiciously kept his left hand behind his back as he closed the door.

"What makes you think I'm hiding something?"

"Show me your hands."

"Okay." He took a step sideways so that he was in front of her Christmas tree and a few seconds later held both hands out for her to inspect.

Gaby lightly pushed him out of the way. "What did you just do?"

"Nothing," he said with pure innocence on his face. It didn't fool her.

Gaby examined her tree. "Oh my goodness." She plopped her hands on her hips as she faced him, trying to look indignant but the pose was ruined by the slight shake of the laughter she was holding back. "I can't believe you tried to get away with that. I am so offended."

Owen shrugged as though he didn't know why she might be offended.

"I see those glitter balls. I thought you were going to let me add some Christmas spirit to your place this year, you Scrooge. We had a deal. Decorations for cookies. What happened?"

"I'm just adding a small stipulation. No glitter."

Gaby glanced at her tree and then back at Owen. "But it's pretty."

"It's a menace."

"What are you talking about?"

"Those two tiny balls of it sat on my plant all weekend. I never touched them and yet... there's glitter everywhere." He moved his arms in large circles to emphasize the word.

"Everywhere?" Gaby narrowed her eyes skeptically.

"Yes, everywhere. I've found it on my hands and on my couch and on my clothes and there was even a speck of glitter on my dinner plate last night. I almost ate your Christmas spirit."

Gaby laughed as she said, "I think you're making things up, but I'll let you get away with it... this time."

The playful expression on her face made Owen wonder what else he could get away with. He needed to keep his mind where it was allowed to go. "So what's going on with the boxes over here?" he asked. He gestured to two cardboard boxes that seemed to have exploded in Gaby's living room. The flaps were open and various stacks of papers surrounded the room.

"My mom insisted I take two more when I was at their house yesterday."

"More school papers?"

"Mostly," Gaby said. Her mom saved everything. She was trying to get Gaby to store her childhood items in her apartment. Gaby took the boxes as they were offered but ended up keeping very little from each one. "It's like from elementary school. There are a lot of simple worksheets and most of this stuff is really boring. You have to see this story I wrote in third grade though." Gaby looked around for it as she talked. "It's the most disturbing fairy tale you've ever read. There's an evil queen and she had a baby boy. Then forty years later she has a baby girl, which I don't even think

17

is possible, and then forty years after that she somehow tricks her children into marrying each other."

"That sounds… um…" Owen shook his head as he clearly couldn't come up with a word more appropriate than disturbing.

Gaby found the handwritten story. It had a queen with an overly large smile drawn in crayon on the side. She handed it to Owen. His eyebrows jumped up after he read a few sentences and they stayed there while he finished. He read the last sentence out loud. "'And the evil queen had everything she ever wanted. The end.' Wow."

"Exactly." Gaby took the paper back and tried to decide where she wanted to put it. "I bet Mrs. Gully got a laugh out of it."

"You had Mrs. Gully in third grade? Me, too."

Gaby looked thoughtful. "That's right. I remember you used to dominate at Around the World."

"Around the World?"

"Yeah. That was the game with the math flash cards."

"Oh, I remember that. I don't remember dominating."

"You were good."

"There are probably a lot of things about third grade that I've forgotten. I think you might be able to piece together the whole year here though." Owen gestured to the stacks of paper.

Gaby rolled her eyes. "I can't believe my mom saved most of this stuff. Look, here's a spelling test from second grade." She held up a small lined paper.

"Ten out of ten," Owen observed.

"I still don't need to keep it." Gaby put it back on the pile.

"You're going to throw out everything here?"

"I'll probably hang on to that freaky story and maybe a few other things. Most of it is scrap though."

"Can I ask you a question then?"

"What?"

"Why are you sorting it if it's garbage?"

Gaby cast her eyes over the papers that she had been carefully sorting by grade and subject and then shrugged sheepishly. "Apparently my mom's hoarding genes are trying to take over my common sense. I didn't think about what I was doing."

"So we can shove the stacks on the couch together for a TV break?"

"Um…"

Owen stopped before he touched any of the papers and laughed at her hesitation. "Those are some powerful genes."

"Stop laughing at me. I'm only sorting it to help me decide if there's anything worth keeping. I can move it." She picked up all her stacks from the couch and put them in one big stack on the kitchen table. Owen didn't say anything about the way she alternated the piles to make them easy to separate later. He sat and pulled up her list of recorded shows.

"Hang on a sec," Gaby said as she claimed the middle seat. A male friend would have sat on the opposite end of the couch. "We have one important item to discuss before you start something."

"Okay," Owen said slowly. He had a feeling this important business had to do with her Christmas preparations.

"I've decided that Saturday is cookie-making day and I need to know if you're committed to helping or if I need to try to recruit someone else."

"Isn't it a little early for Christmas cookies?"

"I didn't think you ever thought it was too early for cookies."

"Not for eating them."

"Well," Gaby said, "I need to get mine passed out before everyone already has gobs of competing goodies. So are you going to help or not?"

Owen almost shook his head because he didn't want to make cookies. But then he remembered what Jimmy had said about making romantic gestures. Did agreeing to help with something Christmasy send a signal that he cared about making Gaby happy or that he was a pushover?

When Gaby realized she wasn't getting the immediate no she'd expected, her face lit up and she said, "Oh, please… it'll be fun. I have good Christmas music we can listen to and I'll get extra sprinkles and it'll be fun. Please."

Owen smiled in slight defeat. He couldn't disappoint her now no matter what signal it might send. "All right," he said. "What time?"

"That depends. Do you want to shop for ingredients with me?"

"No," Owen said, glad that she made the shopping sound optional. He could help without being a complete pushover.

"Okay. In that case, come over right after lunch." She grinned and nearly danced with excitement.

"I'll put it on my calendar."

"Good. And if you forget, I know where to find you."

"I guess that means I can't pretend to forget."

Gaby feigned shock. "You would never do that to me."

Owen tried to look as though he was considering it. "How long is this cookie making supposed to take anyway?"

"We'll have so much fun that you'll be sorry when it's over no matter how long it takes."

"How long will it take?" he asked again.

She smiled. "Don't worry."

Owen sighed and picked a show to watch. They talked about it only for a minute when it was over and then Owen said he should head back to his place.

Gaby slipped on some shoes and followed him out the door. He eyed her suspiciously as she unhooked the fluffy red wreath from her door and took it over to hang on his. He said nothing as she performed this operation and waved as she returned happily to her side of the building.

"Goodnight, Owen."

Chapter 3

When Gaby got home from work the next day she didn't immediately notice what had happened. She had already unlocked her door when she realized that her wreath had been returned. She smiled to herself as she took the wreath down and put it back on Owen's door. After she got comfortable, she sent him a text that said: You're a mean one, Mr. Grinch.

She had finished her dinner and gone back to sorting her piles of papers when her phone buzzed a text. Owen had replied: You've had that wreath for years. When it's on my door, it looks like I stole it.

She rolled her eyes at his excuse and typed out: No one thinks you stole my wreath.

A minute later she heard scraping noises on her front door that probably meant her wreath was being returned again. She marched over and opened the door. Owen offered an apologetic smile but there was defiance in his eyes, as if he was daring her to keep trying to give him decorations. Gaby stared right back. She was going to have to think about how to meet that challenge. But she had a different priority at the moment. "Get in here," she said.

Owen laughed as he came inside. "That is the most polite invitation you have ever issued."

"Sorry. Please do me the honor of entering my humble home." Gaby turned to Owen as she closed the door and he seemed to be waiting for something. "Do I need to yell at you about the wreath or do you already feel bad about not accepting it?"

"I told you that—"

"Is that really the best defense you can come up with? That other people are keeping track of whose door it's on?"

"Did you bring me inside just to yell at me about the wreath?"

"No actually." Gaby grinned and pointed to her kitchen table. "I got a batch of Santa letters!"

"I told you I wasn't going to help," Owen said as he made a

21

move for the door.

Gaby stepped sideways to block him. "You don't have to help. You just hang out with me while I answer the letters and maybe occasionally make suggestions."

"That sounds like helping."

Gaby didn't say anything. She started walking towards her table with the waiting letters while she motioned to Owen like she was coaxing a shy kitten out of hiding.

He followed slowly as he said, "I'll sit with you. But if you try to hand me a pen, I'm leaving."

Gaby picked up a red slip of paper from her table and passed it to Owen. "They finally updated the rules this year. It's hilarious."

He took it and began to read. The Santa letters were an elementary school fundraiser. Kids paid to write letters to Santa and they were answered by volunteers. Gaby had been one of those volunteers since she was in high school. The sheet of instructions had been exactly the same – except that the photocopies got more and more distorted and off-center – each of her previous years. "Look how many exclamation points come after 'Do not make any promises.'"

Owen nodded before he read aloud, "Do not, under any circumstances, inform a child that Santa does not exist." He looked up. "Is that difficult for you to follow?"

"Of course not. I'm not a fantasy-killer."

"Yeah. Explain to me again how you justify promoting the myth you don't agree with." Owen sat at the table and leaned back in the chair as he dropped the red paper.

Gaby glared at him. "Don't make it sound like I'm some sort of hypocrite. It's complicated."

"Complicated?" His tone and his expression revealed skepticism. "You don't remember believing in Santa. You don't want your own kids to believe in Santa. You think the stories some people make up to convince their kids that he's real are ridiculous. And yet you're helping by pretending to be Santa."

"I'd explain again if I thought you really wanted to understand," Gaby said with an exaggerated sigh. This was already feeling like the conversation they'd had each of the last three years.

"Go ahead," Owen said, "tell me again how you *are* Santa."

"Fine. We are all Santa." Gaby took a seat opposite Owen and pulled a handful of kids' letters from a manila envelope while she ignored her friend's laughter.

"I'm not trying to make fun of you," Owen said, not entirely convincingly. "I just really don't get it."

"All right. I don't believe in Santa as some magical person but as a symbol of the spirit of giving that we all have. There's nothing wrong with writing responses that encourage kids to appreciate the power of... to at least begin to appreciate the gift of giving. I think Santa represents a form of love." She smiled teasingly. "Like the love you'll feel when you pick out an especially huge and expensive present for me this year."

"I only love you for your cookies."

"The cookies you're going to help me make this year?"

It looked for a moment as though Owen might consider trying to back out of being a cookie helper, or was at least going to give her a hard time about his having been forced into it, but he nodded towards the letters in Gaby's hand instead and said, "Let me see some of those."

She passed him the first letter.

"This is not a letter," he said. "It's a shopping list."

"I know. Some of them are harder to work with than others. But as you can see from the carefully worded instructions, the idea is to restate some of the gift ideas for the parents to see. We can do that while we compliment the kid on his good taste in toys, give him a reason he might not get the things he wants, and tell him how much Santa likes being able to give presents. That last part is the most important. Planting the seed of the idea that giving makes you feel good."

Owen handed the letter back. "I guarantee you take this more seriously than any of the other volunteers."

"And I bet I enjoy it more, too."

"Can I see another one?"

Gaby passed Owen the rest of the letters while she began to work on her answer for the first. He alternated between reading the letters and watching her work. Something about his demeanor said that he couldn't help respecting what she was trying to do even while he couldn't make any sense of it. That was why Owen was the only person to whom she'd ever tried to explain her theory of Santa.

23

"Oh, no," she heard him mumble.

"What?"

"I don't know how you're going to answer this one." He handed her the letter he'd just read. "It's sad."

The letter was from a 7-year-old boy whose dad had just moved out of the house. He said having his family back together was the only thing he wanted for Christmas. Gaby sighed. That would be a difficult one to answer. She'd do that one later. "Give me an easy one," she said to Owen.

"Here's a girl who wants a Barbie and all the accessories you can fit in the sleigh."

"That's more like it." Gaby took the letter and prepared a quick response.

She was nearly done when Owen began to read a letter out loud. "Dear Santa, I am fourteen years old. I know that is too old to believe in you. I do anyway. Please write back and tell me I'm right. Also, I want a pink tricycle for Christmas. And a Cinderella dress." He smiled at Gaby.

She rolled her eyes. "There's one every year. Some kid who thinks it's funny to write a letter and sign someone else's name."

"It says it's from Zander Daw."

"Yeah. I figured it'd be a boy's name. Hence the need to specify a *pink* tricycle." Gaby grabbed a piece of answer stationery and tapped the table with her pen while she thought.

"Are you going to yell at someone for not taking this seriously?" Owen was clearly not taking it seriously either.

"No. Someone paid to have Zander get a funny response. I'll do my best to give him what he wants. Dear Zander," she said as she wrote the name. "I was so happy to receive your letter. I have only one Cinderella gown in your size left this year. I'll see if my elves can add a few more sequins before we wrap it. I hope you will take a picture of yourself in the gown and send it to me next year. Thank you for telling me how much you love me and be sure to thank the person who helped you write to me. This letter has been a true gift. Santa."

When Gaby looked up, Owen was watching her with a strange expression. Something about it made her blush.

"What?" she asked.

"I'm impressed that you're playing along."

24

"Are you suggesting I'm not usually a good sport?"

"Of course not," Owen said. "I just figured you'd be upset with the kid for messing with Christmas."

"He's having fun with it. I think that's wonderful."

"As long as Zander shares his sense of humor."

Gaby considered the point. "I think I made it clear that I knew the first letter was a joke. That should keep him from being embarrassed by it. Don't you think?"

"Yeah." He shoved the rest of the letters back towards Gaby. "Is it time for a break?"

"I've only answered three of the ten letters."

"That's a good start."

She narrowed her eyes at him. "I'm trying to be responsible here."

"That says you have eight more days. You're already ahead of schedule."

"You're supposed to be helping me."

"I'm pretty sure I said I was not helping." Owen looked up as though he needed to check his memory. "Yeah, I did say not helping. How about we play *Qwirkle* at the same time? Then I can complain that *you're* taking too long for a change."

"Fine," Gaby said. "But I don't complain. I simply remind you that we're playing a game when it seems like you might have forgotten."

Owen had already walked across the room to pick up the game and was bringing it back to the table. "You don't complain?" he said. "This is you. Owen, are you going to take a turn today? Why do you have to take forever? There's only six tiles to choose from. Please play something already. Will you hurry up?"

His impression made Gaby laugh. "Why do you want to play if I complain so much?"

He grinned. "Because I win."

"You don't always win."

"I win more than you do."

"Well, I'm distracted today so that's my excuse if I don't do well." She gestured to the letters around her side of the table.

"No excuses allowed," Owen said as he set up the game.

Gaby wrote another Santa response and then they played. She did a pretty good job distracting Owen with her side task so that the game was slow. There was more asking whose turn it was than complaining about slow turns and it was late by the time they put all the pieces back in the box. But Gaby did finish all ten letters before they called it a night, even the sad one.

"Should I pick up another batch of letters for us to do tomorrow?" she asked.

"No way." Owen shook his head.

"Thanks for your help with these anyway."

He opened his mouth to say something but seemed to realize that he had been helping even though he hadn't intended to do so. He sighed. "I'm getting out of here before you turn me into an elf."

Gaby smiled as he opened the door but was reminded of the returned wreath when she saw it. "Wait," she said. "Take, um, take this for your apartment." She pulled a felt candy cane from her tree.

Owen just looked at it.

"It's small. And there's no glitter."

"I don't have a tree to hang it on." Owen took the candy cane. "Oh, wait, here's one." He hung it back on Gaby's tree.

She tried to frown at him as she said goodnight but she knew she'd made it too easy on him. She looked over her apartment trying to think of the perfect decoration for the next time she visited him, something he couldn't think of a reason to return. If only the knitting had turned out.

Gaby had recently decided to teach herself to knit. A few weeks before Thanksgiving, she had begun to make a stocking for Owen. There was no way he was heartless enough to refuse a handmade decoration, especially if she put his name on it. The stocking attempt, however, had been an amazing failure. The toe was misshapen and a hole appeared in the side that got larger the more she tried to fix it. She had stuffed the project under her couch in disgust.

She sat now and slid it out to examine. It was worse than she remembered. But it gave her an idea. The one thing she knew she could make was a scarf. If she used the red and green yarn to make Owen a scarf, he could take the holiday cheer with him wherever he went. Gaby moved a stack of fraction worksheets to the floor to make room for her knitting supplies. It was too late now but she'd get started pulling apart the awful stocking the next chance she got. And she looked forward to feeling like Santa as she worked the yarn into something better.

****

"Gabrielle, did you see that woman who was in a little while ago?"

"You'll have to be more specific," Gaby said without looking up.

"She had blonde hair and a long wool coat."

"I don't think I saw her."

"Well, anyway, she had her nails done in this bubble gum pink color and she had to be at least forty. It was way too young for her."

"Hmm."

"Oh, Gabrielle, Kevin's mom brought over this pot pie last night that was so good. I had so much I know I must have gained a pound or two. I brought the leftovers for lunch."

"Speaking of lunch," said a new, deeper voice, "where do you disappear to every day?"

Gaby looked up to see Jared Greener standing in front of her. He seemed to be making a habit of sneaking up on her while she was trying to appear busy. She smiled at him. "It's no secret. I live three blocks away and think it's easier to go home for lunch than to decide what I'll feel like having when it's still morning."

"I can understand that. I live in Port Harris. If I went home I'd spend the whole hour getting there and back and have no time to eat."

"That sounds like a rough commute."

Jared shrugged. "I don't mind it. But about lunch…" He glanced at Krista for a moment and Gaby noticed that she was watching attentively. "Krista and I," he continued, "were talking yesterday and we agreed that we should talk you into joining us in the break room sometime. What would it take to convince you to pack a lunch tomorrow?"

Gaby tapped her finger against her chin as though this was a matter that required serious consideration. She tried to ignore the strange feeling that Jared was trying to appear interested in her

27

rather than actually being interested. That didn't matter if she was only being asked to join coworkers for lunch. It was not a date. "I guess," she said, "that I could make an exception if entertainment will be provided."

"Does watching me try not to drip anything on my tie count as entertainment?"

"No, but I guess I can come anyway. If I don't forget."

"I'm counting on you not forgetting," Jared said. He waved at Krista as he returned to his office.

"Gabrielle, this is great. I already told him that you were interested and that you weren't seeing anyone."

Gaby's stomach twisted as though she'd already had lunch and something in it was still alive as she turned to Krista. "What else did you tell him?"

"Oh, let's see. I told him that you're twenty-five and that you've lived in Hartford your whole life and that you almost never talk about yourself so I couldn't give him any more details. Gabrielle, you should really talk about yourself more."

Gaby was grateful for her natural tendency towards privacy. She studied Krista for a moment while she tried to decide if it was worth explaining that she hadn't yet determined if she was interested in more than flirting with Jared. The front door ushered in a few customers and Krista landed on a different topic as soon as they departed.

Chapter 4

Gaby almost forgot lunch the next morning. She had to run back up the stairs to find something to bring with her. There was something in her freezer with rice that would work. It was already in a box so she didn't need a bag.

Krista led her back to the break room as though Gaby was a brand new employee. A few other coworkers noted surprise that she was staying. It wasn't the first time, but it had probably been at least six months. Gaby hadn't realized that the change in her routine might generate speculation. She hoped Krista was the only one who knew it had anything to do with the new guy. And though it was likely unrealistic, she hoped Krista would keep it that way.

They sat at a small round table in the corner. There were two guys at a nearby table discussing a recent football game and an older woman across the room reading a book while she ate from a large bag of chips. Krista said, "Jared's been getting something from the sandwich place next door. He'll be here soon."

Gaby nodded nonchalantly while she opened her lunch. She squinted at the directions on the back to determine whether or not to cut the plastic before putting it in the microwave, which had a sign on the front that read, "PLEASE clean up after yourself if something explodes in here." When her food was warm, and still in its container, she sat next to Krista. Jared came in and sat on her other side before she had her first bite.

"You remembered," he said.

"Yes, I did," she answered simply.

The three employees sat eating quietly for a few moments. The guys at the next table were fairly animated, and distracting.

"Krista tells me that you've lived in Hartford your whole life," Jared said. He somehow made it sound like an invitation for Gaby to share her entire life story.

She said, "Mostly."

He tried again. "What does mostly mean?"

"It means almost all."

Jared smiled but Krista sighed heavily. "He wants to know when you didn't live in Hartford," she said. "And so do I."

"Well, I went away for college. But it was still close enough that I was home for the summers and a lot of breaks. I've never missed Christmas in Hartford."

"What did you study at school?" Jared asked.

Gaby bit her lip. "Elementary education."

"You have a degree in teaching?" Krista said as she put down her fork and looked at Gaby as though she had suddenly begun a break dance routine. "What are you doing working at a bank?"

Gaby found this bit of her history mildly embarrassing and Krista's reaction didn't help. Jared, however, simply looked like someone expecting an interesting story. Gaby focused on him while she tried to explain. "I thought I wanted to be a teacher when I started school. I started having doubts right away, but I kind of ignored them. It was sometime in my third year when I had to admit that teaching just wasn't the job for me. By then there was no other degree I could finish in four years, and maybe not even five. I didn't want to keep going into debt if there wasn't something else I particularly wanted to do. I thought about dropping out but… I don't know, I like to finish things and it just seemed like having a degree was better than not having a degree even if I wasn't going to really use it."

"And what made you want to be a teller?" Jared asked.

Gaby shrugged. "The only thing I knew for sure was that I wanted to live in Hartford. There aren't a lot of options in a small town. But I mostly like this job now that I have it."

"You must love it," Krista said. "I don't know how else you could stand to be at any job for as long as you have."

"Do you have siblings?" Jared asked.

"I have two sisters."

"Older or—"

"What about you?" Gaby said before Jared could finish. If they were going to play Twenty Questions, she wanted to get in her share. "How long have you lived in Port Harris?"

"Around four years."

"Were you a loan officer there?"

Jared nodded.

"What made you want the longer commute to the Hartford Bank?"

"I felt like a change of scenery."

"See," Krista said, "normal people like to change jobs now and then."

Gaby was still watching Jared. It may have been her imagination, but she got the impression that his answer was less than the whole truth. He kept his eyes on his sandwich and took a large bite. Gaby concentrated on her lunch as well. Krista was listing a few other jobs she'd had. When she took a break, Jared tried to bring the conversation back to Gaby.

"This sandwich isn't bad. What can you, as a local, tell me about the other places to eat in town?"

"You've probably figured out The Sandwich Shoppe is the only fast food we have and it's okay for lunch. But if you want a good meal, the two best places are Pops and Fred's."

"Oh, we've had Pops," Krista said. "They make good pizza."

Gaby nodded. "It's delicious. And Fred's has generic, you know, typical American food for the most part and a lot of it is great."

"I'll need to get Kevin to take me there. He's too lazy to go out most of the time. He likes Pops because they deliver."

Jared smiled. "They probably don't deliver to Port Harris, do they?"

"Nope," Krista said, "you'll have to get Gaby to invite you to her place."

Gaby said nothing. She didn't think it would do any good to point out to Krista that her comment was out of line. Jared also said nothing. But he nodded at Krista as though he was considering her idea.

Gaby didn't need anyone to flirt for her. She needed a new topic. "Hartford's Christmas tree lighting is this Sunday."

"Oh, boy." Krista waved a finger in the air in fake enthusiasm.

"What's that like?" Jared at least mustered interest, if not excitement.

"There's a really big evergreen at the park. They're already working on getting the decorations up and then they'll switch it on for the first time Sunday night."

"Is that it?" His interest appeared to be waning.

31

"They have hot chocolate and Christmas carols."

"Fascinating," Krista said with an eye roll.

Gaby's lunch was finished so she stood to throw out her trash. She hadn't really intended to sign up for more time with Krista. "I'm going to stretch my legs a bit before I go back to work," she said.

Her companions nodded at her and she grabbed her jacket to walk around the block. The weather had warmed up again since the night of Santa's arrival and she almost didn't need the jacket. She reentered through the back door and Jared was in his office as she walked past it. She smiled at him and he waved his hand in an invitation for her to enter.

Gaby stepped inside the door and he stood. "Hi," he said.

"Hello. Sorry I ran out on lunch a little early."

"I understand," he said. Then he walked around his desk and sat against the front of it. He was a little farther away than he had been in the break room, but he felt closer because there was no table and no Krista between them. "How was your walk?" he asked.

"Quiet. Did you call me in here to ask about my walk?"

"Maybe," he said with a sly smile. "Was your walk... lonely?"

Gaby felt her face heat up. She was at work. She needed to keep the conversation suitable for the setting. "It was quiet," she repeated.

Jared continued to smile at her for a moment. Then he switched suddenly to a serious expression. "Look, I know you need to get back to work so I'll just be honest. I'd like to ask you out. Maybe we could go to Pops after work one night this week. I hear their pizza is delicious and we could have an uninterrupted conversation. What do you say?"

Gaby smiled. "I think I'd say yes."

"Excellent. Are you busy Friday?"

"That's tomorrow."

"So it is."

"No, I'm not busy."

"Good. We have a date."

"Good." Gaby hoped her expression as she returned to her station didn't betray what had just happened. She didn't want anyone to notice how excited she was at the prospect of a date, something she hadn't had in what felt like a very long time. And she didn't want Krista to notice anything.

****

Owen didn't have a regular lunch routine. He knew that Gaby ate late because the bank was busy during other people's lunch hour. If he was also running late, he would go home and try to bump into Gaby. Other times he picked up something to eat in town or packed a lunch, which usually went uneaten if he thought he had a chance to bump into Gaby.

On that same Thursday that Gaby stayed at the bank, Owen ate quickly in his office and then went out for a non-food errand. There was a store in Hartford called "Things to Do." He knew the owner slightly because she was one of his sister's friends in high school. He hadn't talked to her much since then, but she'd gained a reputation in the last few years as a person with answers. Her hobby store filled voids people hadn't realized existed. As there weren't a lot of places to shop in Hartford, people initially walked into her store out of desperation. But Jill always seemed to have exactly what was needed.

Owen grabbed the door handle and resisted the impulse to cover his ears at the clanging that ensued to announce his arrival. A woman with light purple hair and a basketball-shaped stomach rose slowly from a stool in the corner. "Owen," she said, "I haven't seen you in forever. How's Ava?"

"Good. She just had her first baby two months ago. When are you due?"

Jill sighed. "Ten days ago."

"Wow. I don't know much about pregnancy but isn't that…"

"Horribly uncomfortable? Yes. But she's being evicted tomorrow."

"Well, congratulations a day early then."

"Thanks. But as you might have read on the sign there," she pointed towards the front window, "that means I'll be closing up for at least a few days so we should focus on you. Are video games still your passion or have you moved on to something new?"

"I still play but not as much as I used to."

"So you're not here for a game?"

33

Owen shook his head. "I'm not actually sure why I'm here."

"Oh... tricky." Jill looked delighted by the challenge. "You need *something* though, right?"

"I had a thought but it's... vague."

"Come in, come in." Jill motioned for him to move deeper into her store. "Now tell me your thought."

Owen hesitated, partly because he was a little embarrassed and partly because Jill was as nutty as he remembered. She was wearing a short black dress with white polka dots and pink knee socks covered in yellow rubber ducks. Her eyes moved from him to various shelves around them as though she wanted to be ready to seize something for him. "Okay," Owen started, "I think I want some sort of Christmas project."

"This is not for you, is it?"

"No. I know someone. She's always working on something. She likes to organize things and... last year she bought a harmonica on a whim and taught herself to play a couple of songs and... it just feels like she always has some sort of project. And I think she likes Christmas more than anything so I thought... maybe if I could combine those ideas there'd be a present there."

Jill nodded slowly. "I'm getting the picture now. The first thing that comes to mind when you say Christmas project... I have a few needlepoint kits with holiday themes. There's a wreath and... but you don't want one of those."

"I don't?" Owen had thought that sounded promising.

Jill shook her head. "Definitely not. I also have over here..." She turned and walked back towards the front of her store. Owen followed uncertainly. She picked up a box and handed it to him. It was a kit for building a gingerbread house. Then she took it away from him and said, "We need to put that back."

"I don't know. That's—"

"It's not right," Jill said definitively. She looked lost in thought and Owen tried to wait patiently. Then her face spread into a very wide grin. "I have paper."

Owen didn't know what that meant. He followed her to an aisle on the side anyway. Jill picked up a package of red construction paper and held it for a minute. Then she picked up some green and handed both to Owen. "And white," she said as she handed him a third package.

34

"Um, what do I do with this?" he asked.

"Cut it into strips and make a paper chain."

Owen stared at Jill. He didn't want to offend her but he was sure her other ideas had been much better. "Are you sure this is—"

"Write on the strips," she said as she held her hand up to cut him off. "That's all I'm going to tell you. Write on the strips and it will be perfect."

The paper didn't cost much and Owen thought they might sell gingerbread house kits at the Market. He told Jill he'd take the paper. She added a roll of clear tape before he paid for it and he went back to work wondering what he was going to do with a hundred and fifty sheets of construction paper.

He did stop at the Market after work. He did not buy anything with gingerbread while he was there. He looked at some kits, but they didn't feel right. Gaby was going to spend hours making cookies from scratch. Why would she want an inferior store-bought treat? Owen picked up a few items for dinner instead. He hadn't cooked for Gaby in a few days and she might be expecting a dinner invitation. That might make up for returning her wreath.

He stalled until Liz took over at the register. Liz tended to focus on the job. She said, "Hello," totaled his purchases quickly and wished him a nice day. This was a stark contrast to what would have happened if Mabel was still working. Mabel was an expert on the lives of everyone in Hartford and kept asking Owen when he was going to buy Gaby a ring no matter how many times he told her they were only friends.

Chapter 5

Gaby opened her freezer when she got home from work and closed it without removing anything. She hoped Owen would offer something better. She worked on his scarf while she waited to hear from him and was surprised when her phone rang. Owen almost always texted. The screen said Hannah.

"Hey, sis," Gaby said as she answered. "What's up?"

"Not much. I started studying for exams today and well, I needed a break already so I thought I'd check in."

"For once I have news. I have a date tomorrow."

"Really? Is it Owen?"

"Of course it's not Owen." There was a queasy feeling in Gaby's gut that felt almost like panic at the idea.

"You're still pretending you're not interested in him, huh?"

"It's better that we're friends. You know it would be hugely awkward living next door to him if something happened and it didn't work out."

"Excuses, excuses," Hannah said with a sigh. "All I'm saying is that you can't make him off limits if you're not going to make a move yourself. It's kind of unfair to the rest of us."

"What do you care? I heard you found someone at school."

"Yeah, speaking of things not working out..."

Gaby winced. "Oh, I'm sorry."

"It's okay. It was mutual. So tell me about this date you have."

"His name is Jared Greener. He's a new loan officer at the bank."

"A loan officer? Is he, like, fifty or something?"

"No! What makes you say that?"

"I don't know. Loan officer just conjures an image of, well, Bob Chapman."

"Ew, Hannah!" Bob Chapman, the bank president, was at least sixty, very round, and had a horseshoe of baldness about his head. He had either given up trying to make the center tuft of hair lie flat or was still waiting for someone to tell him that would be a good idea. It was his abrasive personality that made him unattractive. "I don't know how old Jared is," Gaby said, "but he can't be more than early thirties or so. And he has amazing eyes."

"I guess I'll have to wait 'til I see him."

"Maybe. This is only our first date."

"So you might be done with him by the time I get home?"

"Did you talk to Mom about that, by the way?"

"About what?"

"Apparently Jess told her that you two were staying an extra week and she thinks that means you're not coming home for Christmas at all. She was kind of freaking out about it on Sunday."

"How does staying past exams mean the same as not coming home at all?"

"I don't know. I guess it's a mom thing."

"We're driving home on the 20th," Hannah said. "I'll tell Mom... though I assume Jess already did."

"Okay. I'll plan on heading to Mom and Dad's that afternoon so I can meet you."

"Great. We'll see you soon then. I better hit the books."

Gaby put down her phone thinking that it would be nice to see her sisters again. She didn't exactly feel left out, but she knew Jessica and Hannah were much closer to each other than either of them was to Gaby. All three of them suspected – though their parents refused to confirm or deny – that Hannah had been a surprise addition to the family. There was about four years between Gaby and Jessica and only eleven months between Jessica and Hannah.

Gaby's sisters were sharing an apartment near the college where they were in their third and fourth years of studying chemistry, a subject Gaby hadn't even come close to considering as a major. They thought Gaby was crazy for wanting to spend the rest of her life in Hartford, while Gaby thought she could be very content there if only Owen would make her some dinner.

She picked up her phone again to make sure she hadn't missed anything. Usually if he was going to offer food he'd have done it by now. She considered contacting him. It wouldn't be the first time she invited herself over, but she had already talked him into making cookies and didn't want to be too pushy. She'd give him five more minutes.

He called after only two.

"Gaby," he said, "did you eat yet?"

"No. Is that an invitation?"

"I meant to text you when I got home and then I was wondering why it was taking you so long to come over when I realized that I hadn't actually invited you."

"Good thing I read your mind and waited. I'll be right there."

Gaby had walked to her door while she was talking. She picked up a Christmas offering on her way out the door and held it behind her back while she knocked.

Owen grinned as he let her in. "You were expecting an invitation, huh? How long before you popped over without one?"

"I'm not saying I would have done that, but it has been a long time since you've gone a whole week without cooking for me. It would only be natural for me to be concerned that maybe something had happened to you."

"Right. You'd have come over to make sure I wasn't trapped under something heavy, not because you were hungry."

"Exactly. But it's all moot now. And look what I brought." Gaby pulled a large red bow from behind her and held it up. "No glitter and it has never been on the outside of my apartment so no one will think you took it from me. And you can't pretend you think that anyone else thinks you took it from me."

Owen scrutinized the bow for a moment and seemed to decide that its threat level was minimal. He motioned Gaby into the next room. "Come on," he said. "You can tie it to something in the kitchen while I finish up."

Gaby followed. "Ooh… tacos."

"Yeah, I just need to get the tomatoes cut up."

"I'll decorate while you do that." She looked around the room and decided to tie the bow to the top of the handle on his freezer. Then she took a red glitter ball out of her pocket. She eyed him carefully to make sure his attention was on the tomatoes before she slipped the small ornament onto the back of his counter, partially hidden by some cereal boxes.

He glanced at her a moment later and said, "What's so funny?"

"Nothing. Just excited about the tacos."

Owen looked doubtful but he didn't ask again. Gaby tried to squelch the smile while she watched him. The dress code where he worked was more relaxed. He typically got away with plain T-shirts. Today, however, he was wearing a blue button front shirt. He looked good in it... too good. Gaby stared hard at the red bow she'd brought over as she tried to ignore the unwanted attraction.

When she turned back to Owen, he was sliding the chopped tomatoes into a bowl. The cuffs of his sleeves were unbuttoned and pushed back and she noticed a gash on his left forearm, the arm closer to her. "Ouch," she said. "What did you do to your arm?"

He glanced down. "Oh, I was working with some cables yesterday and I reached under a desk without realizing there was a bolt sticking out down there."

"It looks painful. I didn't know IT was a dangerous job."

"I think I'll live. You ready to eat?"

Gaby nodded and helped him bring everything to the table. Owen said a brief prayer. As they put together their tacos, Gaby said, "It's a good thing we're doing this today because I won't be able to join you tomorrow. I have a date."

Owen didn't respond right away and Gaby was worried that he didn't want to hear about her date. That would be bad. She didn't want anything awkward between them and it hadn't been weird before. But then he said, "I see what you did," and she realized that he was looking at the glitter ball she'd left on his counter.

"I thought if you didn't know there was glitter then you wouldn't imagine it getting all over the place and your apartment could still be a touch more Christmasy."

"So I wasn't supposed to notice that?"

She shook her head and took a bite of the taco. It was yummy.

"Doesn't it sort of defeat the purpose of decorations to put them where people can't see them?"

She pretended she couldn't answer because her mouth was full. She didn't want to admit that he might have a good point.

"Is your date the new guy at the bank?"

"Yes. We're going to Pops after work."

"Pops is good."

"Always. Though I think it's been too long for me to remember what the pizza tastes like on a date."

39

Owen narrowed his eyes slightly. "The pizza tastes the same."

"Mostly," Gaby said. "But the excitement of a date, the possibilities you know, that changes everything a little bit."

"If you say so."

"It's sort of like Christmas. Things are just happier… better… when it's Christmas."

"I've gathered that you're a fan of the holiday." Owen was trying not to laugh.

"I'm going to convert you, too… eventually. I'm making something for you."

Owen looked at her in anticipation.

"I'm not going to tell you. It's a surprise."

"Then I'm not going to tell you what I bought today."

"You bought something? For me?" Gaby grinned. Her eyes shimmered and began moving around the room in an eager search for something new.

"It's…" He shook his head as though he didn't know what to say.

"Is it something Christmasy?" Gaby asked.

"Sort of."

"I'm converting you already." She turned around to cast her eyes over the connected living room. "I don't see any decorations so it's not a decoration, right?"

Owen shrugged. "Not really."

"Sort of and not really? What kind of answers are those? Do you even know what you bought?"

"Not exactly," he said with another faltering shake of his head.

Gaby stopped asking questions and simply worked on him with a confused stare.

"Okay," he said, "I went to 'Things to Do' today. I thought maybe I could find some kind of fun Christmas thing and Jill did have an idea, but I'm not sure… you might not like it."

"Jill is pretty good. Remember last year when I almost forgot to get my mom a birthday present. Jill suggested those vintage picture frames and Mom loved them. She had a blast refinishing them and now they're like the centerpiece of the family room."

"I'll let you be the judge but not today."

"Why not today?"

"I want my surprise at the same time."

40

"Hmm…" Gaby tapped her fingers against the table as she thought. "If I work hard Sunday afternoon, I can probably finish it before the tree lighting. You are going to the tree lighting, aren't you?"

Owen shrugged. "I thought I'd see what the weather's like."

Gaby opened her mouth to protest his lack of enthusiasm. She stopped herself with a reminder that he was already going to make cookies with her and had apparently just bought something Christmasy. That was excellent progress on her Grinchy friend. "Okay," she said, "I'll go to the tree lighting by myself. Can you come over after I get back?"

"Sure."

"Bring your surprise and I'll have mine ready. I hope."

"Now don't get your hopes up too much."

"Same to you," Gaby said, thinking that her stitches were not lying as flat as she would like.

She stayed for some TV after dinner and when she mentioned a show that Owen could definitely watch without her, he made a mental note to watch that one while he was trying not to think about how her date was going.

****

Pops had two other names when Gaby was a kid, but it had always been a pizza place. Her parents said that the pizza was best under the current owner. The inside had been recently repainted so that a mural of hot air balloons covered one wall. There were red booths along both sides and tables scattered through the middle.

Jared and Gaby walked there after work. She felt nervous but not jittery as they took a booth. The restaurant was somewhat loud and got more crowded soon after they ordered. So far they had shared only small talk about the office. Gaby had spent part of the day thinking up questions that would be more personal but not too personal. She tried, "Where did you grow up?"

"Tennessee," he said. "Kind of near Nashville."

"And what made you come to Port Harris?"

"A job. I kept waiting tables for a few years after college because it was income, but I had a degree in finance that I actually wanted to use." He paused to smile at her.

41

She nodded that she understood the reference to her unrelated degree.

"And then I was offered a position in Port Harris. It was only supposed to be temporary, but I figured the experience might open some other doors. And then I met... I mean, I was still glad when they let me stay on permanently."

Gaby noticed the change of course in his answer. She assumed he was omitting an ex-girlfriend. Since everyone knew you didn't mention exes on a first date, she let it slide. "Do you still have family in Tennessee?"

"Just my parents. And a few friends."

"Are you going to try to go back for Christmas?"

"I don't know yet. I'd like to. I can't take much time off though so I don't know if the drive will be worth it for such a short stay."

"I guess I'm lucky that my family is close. Even my grandparents live in Hartford. But I'm taking a few days off anyway just because I can."

"I'm glad to hear that," Jared said. "I've known people who refused to take off the time they'd earned unless they had a quote unquote good reason."

Gaby smiled. "I think Christmas is a good reason. I've been saving my time off for it."

"I think I've figured that out about you already." He tilted his head at the silver reindeer pinned to her sweater. "You seem to enjoy the season even more than the average person. Is there a story there?"

"I don't think there's a story. My birthday is close though. It's the 20th. You know how kids get really excited about their birthdays? Well, I think I had all my excitement on that one week of the year and as I got older it all sort of focused on Christmas."

"How old are you?"

"On my birthday, I'll be twenty-six."

"And you've already stopped caring about birthdays?"

"I still care," Gaby said. "I like it when people wish me a happy birthday and everything. But taking two dozen friends to a bounce house in the city would be overkill."

Jared reached into his suit jacket and pulled his phone from an inside pocket. "I'm going to set myself a reminder to wish you a happy birthday."

"Great. Now I'll have something to look forward to."

"I wonder how many times I'll get a chance to say it." He gave her a significant look, one that seemed to say he might see her outside of work again on her birthday. It made her wonder if she'd be able to celebrate with Owen on a different night. He'd made her dinner the previous year and bought a Christmas tree cake from the Market. He stuck twenty-five candles in it and it looked like one of those old-fashioned trees she'd seen in pictures. It was a beautiful memory.

The pizza arrived and the conversation shifted to food for a while, how delicious the pizza was and what other things they liked. Jared asked what movies she'd seen recently and she asked about books. It was fairly typical getting to know each other talk. They walked back to the bank together to retrieve their cars.

"Thanks for the pizza," Gaby said.

Jared nodded as he said, "You're welcome. Do you have weekend plans?"

"I'm making cookies and going to the tree lighting and just diving right into Christmas prep." She was nearly bouncing with the anticipation of the weekend.

"That's right. You mentioned the tree lighting. I'll expect you to tell me how it was on Monday."

"Absolutely. Have a safe drive home."

"You, too," he said with a wave.

Gaby drove the three blocks to her apartment and was already changing into comfortable jammies when she realized there had been no hint of physical contact at the end of the date. She didn't like to rush the first kiss so she wasn't disappointed about that. But when she realized she hadn't even been thinking about it, she knew the evening had at some point stopped feeling like a date. *That* was a disappointment.

Chapter 6

Gaby put some standard groceries into her cart first. Most of
these came from the freezer aisle. Then she pulled out her list of
cookie ingredients and headed to the baking section. She got more
sprinkles than usual. When she was sure she had everything on her
list, she went to the front to pay.

"Good morning, Mabel."

"Hi, hon," Mabel answered as she flicked a long gray braid over
her shoulder. "Did you hear the news? Jack and Jill had a baby girl
yesterday. Helena Grace."

"That's great. Anything else going on?"

"Al Overmeyer's surgery went well. He might be able to come
home tomorrow."

"Also good news. I hope our replacement Santa does a good
job at the tree lighting."

Mabel stopped scanning for just a moment as though
considering the replacement Santa. "I think he's up for it," she
said. "And I hear you got your wreath back. You and the Larrick
boy having some kind of prank war?"

Gaby slowly shook her head. "What do you mean?"

"Oh, he's a good boy. I knew he wouldn't take your wreath to
be malicious."

Something like a snort escaped from Gaby's mouth as she tried
to hold in the laugh. There was no way she was going to tell Owen
that he'd been right about people thinking he stole the wreath. It
must have been a slow week as far as gossip was concerned.
"Honestly," she said to Mabel, "I was trying to share some of my
decorations with him, but he's too much of a Scrooge to keep
them."

"I see you're making cookies. You bring him some of these
first. No man can resist a woman who bakes. After the cookies,
he'll be putty in your hands and you can deck out his side of the
building all you want."

44

Gaby smiled. She said, "I'll try that," rather than admit it hadn't worked yet. "Your husband will be in the bank on Monday as usual, right? Can I send some cookies home with him?"

"Oh, hon, that would be wonderful!"

"I'm not sure if these trays will stack as well as the ones I had last year. I hope I can carry everything."

"You can get one of the men there to help if you need it. Even Bob Chapman will hold a door for a lady if... you know I heard he was thinking about retiring next year."

"Really? Hadn't heard that yet." Gaby was getting her bags back into her cart. She waved to Mabel as she put in the last one and began to make her way to the parking lot. She got a running start as soon as she was outside and jumped onto the back of the cart as it rolled towards her car. She wasn't quite sure what made her do that. The thrill of cookie-making day was stronger than previous years.

She parked in front of her building as her downstairs neighbor was exiting his apartment. Seth Anderson was a huge flirt with adorable dimples to back it up. He'd be dangerous if Gaby hadn't already dated him when she was in high school.

"Gaby, let me help," Seth said as he grabbed several plastic bags from her. He grinned and bumped his eyebrows up and down. "If only I didn't have to go to work. I could spend the whole day *helping* you."

Gaby bit back a laugh. How in the world did the guy make carrying groceries sound suggestive? "Yes, that's too bad, Seth."

"Ooh," he said. "Does that mean you might be free later?"

"I think you missed the sarcasm."

"The only thing I'm missing is the pleasure of your company." He opened his eyes wide in an expression of hope as he gestured for her to go up the stairs first.

She shook her head as she began to climb. "You know I'm not going out with you."

"A guy can dream, can't he?"

Gaby didn't say anything else right away because he seemed to take any conversation as encouragement. She opened her door and dropped her bags inside so she could take the others from Seth. Then she said, "Thanks for your help anyway."

"Anytime. And you have permission to dream about me, too."

45

He flashed those famous dimples and winked as he turned to leave.

Gaby called after him, "Have fun at work."

He waved over his shoulder.

Christmas music was already queued up and Gaby started it as she put away her non-cookie groceries. Then she texted Owen: Time to make COOKIES!!!

He was apparently less eager because he replied with: You said after lunch. It's barely 10 am.

Gaby: I'm ready NOW.

Owen: It's Saturday. I haven't even showered.

Gaby: Hurry up, slowpoke.

Owen: You can't change the plan and then call me slow.

Gaby: I just did.

Owen: I'll come over as soon as I can.

Gaby: And not a minute later.

She got her kitchen table scrubbed and threw an extra sheet over the quilt on her bed. The biggest challenge of cookie day was the scant counter space in her apartment. The cookies would cool on the table and her bed would be a staging area for the trays of finished cookies. She laid out as many trays as would fit and began mixing the first batch of dough. Owen knocked just in time. She was getting ready to roll out the dough and would have been covered in flour a minute later.

His hair was wet and he smelled like soap. It looked as though he might have skipped shaving but his hair was so light it didn't leave much of a shadow. Gaby thought about touching his face to see if his cheek was rough. The thought produced an image in her head of then trying to bring his face lower for a kiss. That was bad! She couldn't think about kissing Owen and she couldn't think about wanting to kiss Owen. They were friends.

Fortunately, he was too distracted by the mess in her living room to notice that his appearance had unnerved her. "Is your closet broken?" he asked.

"No. I was feeling like I was in a clothes rut yesterday and I pulled things out to try to maybe match up some different outfits or see if anything good had gotten pushed into the back of the closet. I haven't had a chance to put everything away."

He chuckled softly. "We still have at least an hour before we were supposed to make cookies. You could have picked up all these clothes before you started bugging me."

"No way," Gaby said. "The cookies were calling out to me. Come on." She motioned him into the kitchen and scooped a mound of dough onto her waiting pile of flour.

Owen stood back a bit. "What do I do?"

"Just watch for a minute. I'm going to have you be in charge of putting things in and out of the oven so I don't have to keep washing the flour off my hands."

He nodded and watched her fill two pans with Christmas tree shapes.

"Okay," she said. "Put those in and set the timer for eight minutes."

"Check." Owen did as he was instructed and then looked over Gaby's shoulder. "What shape is that?"

"You don't recognize Santa when you see him?"

"Oh, it's just the face, right? I see it now."

"It does look more like him when they're decorated. I have candy eyes to put on."

"Can we put eyes on the flying reindeer, too?" He held up a cookie cutter in that shape.

Gaby shook her head. "The reindeer are too small for the eyes I have. They'd look really really surprised."

"What's wrong with that?"

"The cookies are supposed to convey Christmas spirit, not shock."

"Maybe the reindeer are shocked at how much Christmas spirit the people eating them will have."

Gaby was mashing her lips together to keep from laughing. She tried to look serious as she faced Owen. "Christmas spirit is natural. It is not shocking."

"Maybe the reindeer are just shocked at being eaten."

"I'll tell you what. We can put eyes on your reindeer. And if there are any left, you can have surprised angels, too."

"Awesome." Owen put down the reindeer he had been absently pretending to fly while they talked and glanced at the timer. "So, um, how did your date go last night?"

Gaby shrugged.

"Oh," Owen said with a wince. "I don't think I'd want to be

the guy on the receiving end of a post-date shrug."

"Well, it wasn't bad but… I guess I'll wait and see if he wants to go out again."

"So you'd give him another chance?"

"Maybe," Gaby said. "I'm afraid we're not going to click though."

"The timer's getting low. Where are your potholders and where do you want me to put these when they come out?"

Gaby smiled to herself as she answered. She knew already that she'd been right about Owen being the best choice to help with the cookies. The friend who had helped two years ago – someone she hadn't spoken with much recently – had spent the whole time complaining that she wouldn't be able to eat any of the cookies because they'd ruin her diet. When Gaby's mom helped the next year, they were done in record time. Penny Bryant hadn't understood that Gaby wanted to enjoy making the cookies, not just get them done.

Owen, on the other hand, talked about how delicious the cookies looked while he complimented her technique. He alternated between serious helping and goofing off. She caught him singing along to her music more than once. They made five types of cookies. The first two were cutouts that would be decorated after they cooled and then they did two simple drop cookie recipes. They also made a large batch of bar cookies and Owen grabbed her hand when she was about to cut them apart.

"I have a suggestion," he said.

"What is it?"

"You can leave this pan as one giant cookie. It will be for me."

"Very funny," Gaby said and tried to pull her hand out of his.

"Okay, I'm kidding. But really, can you go diagonally and make them triangles?"

"They're called bar cookies."

Owen let go of her hand as he sensed she was at least listening. "But they don't have to be bars," he said. "That's boring."

"Triangles are less boring?"

"Yes. Because it's unexpected. They'll taste better."

"Triangle cookies taste better? That's absurd but I'll cut them that way as your reward for helping today."

She studied the pan for a moment to make sure she'd be able to cut triangles of roughly equal sizes. Owen said, "I thought I got a plate of cookies for helping."

"You know I was going to give you cookies whether you helped or not."

"What!?" Owen was clearly faking his surprise. "You mean I've been helping for nothing?"

"Not nothing. You get to tell people you're the reason these are triangles."

He watched her cut the cookies. "That's all the baking now, right?" Owen asked.

Gaby blew out a breath and looked around her kitchen. "Yes. Now for the decorating."

"No. I think now comes a break."

"What?"

"Gaby, it's nearly 3 o'clock and we haven't even had lunch yet. You need to sit down for a minute."

"Oh, yeah. I did get some sandwiches from the deli this morning."

"Sounds good." Owen opened her refrigerator to look for the sandwiches in question. He read the labels and handed the turkey to Gaby.

"Thank you."

They pulled chairs away from the table and ate over their laps because the table was covered in cookies. Once they were fed and cleaned up, Gaby said they should start with the Santa-shaped cookies to see how many eyes would be left for Owen. She mixed up some red frosting for the hats and white for the beard. "Okay, Owen, you're just going to do eyes. Can you handle that?"

He nodded and began to open the package of candy eyes. Gaby frosted the first cookie and laid it on the table. Owen put two eyes on the hat.

Gaby gave him a dirty look. "You know that's not where eyes go."

"But you already put white dots for eyes."

"That's to make the candy stick. That cookie goes in your batch."

"Really?" Owen gave a mischievous smile. "So I get all the cookies that get messed up?"

"Yes. But you get kicked out if you mess them up on purpose."

He laughed. "Got it. I'm going to eat this one now though so you don't forget to give it to me." He picked up the cookie and took a bite. The expression of enjoyment he offered made up for his not taking the Santa faces seriously. He placed the rest of the eyes with careful precision though. The way he kept checking to see if she approved felt almost like he was flirting with her. Gaby was trying not to let her imagination go there. The kitchen was warm enough from having the oven on for hours. She was kind of glad when they moved on to reindeer.

Until Owen said, "What are you doing?"

"I'm frosting a reindeer. What are you talking about?"

"That's pink."

"I know."

"Reindeer are brown." Owen picked up the box of food coloring. "This says we need yellow and blue to make that brown."

Gaby tried to snatch the box out of his hands. "Don't even think about it," she said. "Brown is not a Christmas color."

"But it's a reindeer color." He held the box over his head and out of her reach. "Pink is completely unnatural."

She didn't try to grab for the food coloring. She stepped back instead because she needed to put a little more space between them. That heat of attraction was back. "I don't care," she said. "I always make the reindeer pink."

"And they are always embarrassed by it. Those bugged out eyes will totally make sense now."

"You are the only one getting eyes and the reindeer are going to be fine being pink. If I try to frost these, do you promise not to try to drop food coloring in over my shoulder?"

Owen grinned and shook his head.

"You better not," she said. Gaby carefully frosted two reindeer.

"Am I supposed to be putting sprinkles on these or anything?"

"No. Reindeer look funny with sprinkles."

"But they don't look funny pink?"

"Look, the stockings and the trees will be green and the angels and stars and bells will all be white. Something other than Santa needs to be red."

"That's pink."

"I know. Owen!" When Gaby looked into her pink frosting, there were two tiny drops of yellow in the bowl and she hadn't even

50

seen him do it. She scooped the yellow out and let it plop into her sink. Then she aimed the frosting-covered spatula at Owen. "If you do that again, I'm going to frost *you*."

Owen laughed; he laughed so hard he had trouble standing up. When he caught his breath he said, "I have never seen anyone take cookies so seriously. I promise to behave." He held his hands up in surrender.

Gaby tried not to let on how much she wanted to laugh as well. She continued working and Owen cooperated with her directions, for the most part. He did insist some of the cookies needed a bit more sprinkles than she would have used. But he was probably not the only one who liked extra. They divided the heavily decorated cookies on the trays with the other types and had the last tray tied with ribbon before 7 pm.

"I didn't realize how many cookies you made over here," Owen said as he looked over the stacks. "Who all are you giving them to?"

"I need one for everyone at the bank and one for my parents and both sets of grandparents and my uncle and his kid and a couple of friends. I always make a few extra trays for the people I remember at the last minute and I promised one to Mabel this year and I'll bring one to church tomorrow for the staff there and of course you get one."

"I hope people appreciate the cookies. Some of them probably have no idea how much effort you put in."

Gaby appeared thoughtful. "Most people look happy to get them, but I really do enjoy making them anyway. And I think I had more fun than ever today so thanks for that."

"I hate to admit it, but it was kind of fun."

"See! Last week you told me there was no such thing as fun work." She playfully punched him in the arm.

Owen wanted to say that it wasn't the work that was fun but spending the day with her. The way she'd just touched him and some of the earlier looks had made it feel like a date. He knew it was likely wishful thinking on his part. But those moments seemed to be happening more often and he couldn't help thinking it might lead to something. He wasn't going to give up until she married him or married someone else. And he wasn't going to think about someone else after such a good day.

Chapter 7

Sometimes Gaby rode to church with her parents and sometimes she took her own car. Owen guessed that she was driving that Sunday because he saw her parents already seated when he came in and she wasn't with them. He greeted them and a few other people before he rejoined his parents. Gaby arrived just a minute late in a green dress that looked wonderful on her. He hadn't seen that one in a while and he concluded that her closet project had been a success.

His mom was in a hurry to get home afterwards because she had set the oven timer before they left. Owen gathered his brother and they returned to Hartford for a quick family meal.

The brothers left their parents' house at the same time. They typically shared a brief goodbye on the porch. This time Jimmy sat first and looked up at his brother. "I assume you need to talk."

"Why do you say that?" Owen asked as he leaned against the opposite railing.

"Well, I did hear that Gaby was at Pops with a guy on Friday night."

Owen rolled his eyes. "Mabel?"

Jimmy nodded.

"I'm actually less worried now. I talked to her yesterday and she seems pretty lukewarm on this guy. I think he's going to be easier to wait out than Pete or Mason."

"I hope so."

Pete had been the original problem. Owen was smitten with Gaby right from the spider incident. He'd had no idea the damsel in distress thing could be so appealing before then. He thought perhaps she was also interested when she showed up later to thank him. But then he found out about Pete. Gaby had met him shortly before graduation and they were trying a long distance thing. That relationship fizzled in about three months, which was enough time for Owen to be firmly established as *the friend*. He hoped a little more time together might start to give her different ideas.

But she met Mason instead. He was from Port Harris and she met him at the grocery store of all places, right in the tiny little Hartford Market, in the cereal aisle. Gaby confided to Owen how she had pretended to want something from the top shelf to strike up a conversation. They talked for a while and arranged their first date right there next to the oatmeal.

They went out exactly five times. Owen couldn't help keeping count. Gaby kept the details to herself during that time but couldn't hide the heartache when Mason got bored. Owen wasn't sure whether the urge to strangle the guy was stronger when he was taking Gaby away or when he hurt her by leaving her alone.

It was during that month of Mason that Owen first admitted to Jimmy how he felt about Gaby. He needed some sort of outlet and while someone younger might not have been his first choice, he knew Jimmy could keep a secret better than most people in Hartford.

Now there was Jared. Owen hoped he was right about Gaby being the one who was bored. "Speaking of waiting things out," he said to Jimmy, "I couldn't help but notice that you were talking to Summer and her boyfriend before *and* after church. That's not something you're hoping against is it?"

Jimmy smiled slightly as he shook his head. "No, Summer and Luke are fine with me."

"You sure? You look sort of guilty about something."

"All right. I guess I might be hoping that if I hang around them enough, Summer will get the idea to fix me up with Emma."

"Interesting plan, little brother. I guess I'm not in a position to suggest you ask her yourself."

Jimmy laughed. "Go ahead. I dare you to give me advice on making a move."

"I do hope Summer comes through for you. Maybe she'll invite both of you over and even hang up some mistletoe."

"I wouldn't hate that but… Hey, that's what you need."

"What do I need?"

"Mistletoe. Hang some up and see if Gaby avoids it. Then you'll know if you're wasting your time."

"You don't think hanging mistletoe in my apartment would fall under the category of obvious?"

53

Jimmy checked his watch. He'd be heading to work soon. "You could try to find some," he said.

"What do you mean?"

"I'm sure there's mistletoe hanging up somewhere in town. There might even be some at the tree lighting and you know Gaby will be there."

Owen gestured towards the sky. "It's gonna rain all over that tree lighting. I don't think that's exactly going to put Gaby in the mood."

"Yeah, I'm not excited about working in the rain either," Jimmy said as he stood. "People forget how to drive."

Owen nodded and he and Jimmy went in opposite directions as they walked away from their parents' house. When Owen got home, there was a string of white lights around his railing. He guessed that had something to do with why Gaby had been late for church. He went inside and texted her: I wonder where those lights came from.

Gaby: My guess is Santa.

Owen: You're going to get wet at the tree lighting.

Gaby: You're still not going?

Owen: Still not going.

Gaby: I'll see you after then. Don't forget the surprise.

Apparently Gaby was still looking forward to her Christmas surprise. He didn't want to disappoint her and had been trying to think of something better. He regretted creating buildup for paper. He was now just hoping they could share a laugh over Jill thinking a paper chain was a good idea. The bigger problem of course was that he still needed a birthday present for Gaby. And something for Christmas. Two presents in one week was a lot of pressure for a guy, especially a guy who wanted to give a romantic gift and didn't know if that would be allowed if he even thought of one.

The rain started around 4 o'clock. It was the kind of rain that had clearly settled in for a long winter's night, heavy with no signs of letting up. Owen assumed that there'd be a light turnout for the tree lighting and that it might end early. At least Gaby would likely be surrounded by other die-hards. They flipped the switch at six so he texted her at seven to ask if she'd be heading home soon.

She replied: `I'm already home.`

He thought it was strange that she hadn't let him know. When she didn't send any more messages, he sent: `Do you still want me to come over?`

She sent only: `OK`

Owen walked over to her side of the building and smiled at the familiar red fuzzy wreath. Gaby seemed a little off when she opened her door. There was nothing wrong with her appearance. She looked beautiful as ever in gray yoga pants and a soft pink shirt. She had probably put on something comfortable enough for sleep early to get dry. Her hair was pulled into a high ponytail that made still damp curls cascade all over her head.

"Come on in." Her voice was flat and she sort of slumped onto her couch. "How are your parents?" she asked.

Owen stashed his bag of paper on the floor as he sat next to her. "Fine, I guess. They want me to drive to Georgia with them for Christmas."

"Ava's definitely not coming home then?"

"Yeah. They're coming home for the Baptism at the end of January and she doesn't want to make the trip twice in a row."

"They can't move the Baptism a few weeks earlier?"

Owen put up his hands. "I'm not involved in the planning. I only know Ava's staying put and Mom wants to see the first grandkid's first Christmas. Jimmy said he'd see if he could get some time off work. I already have that week off, but I'm not wild about the full day's drive there and back. It'll be cramped with all four of us in their car and it doesn't make sense for me to drive by myself if we're all going."

"You should be with family for Christmas though."

"We'll be together in January. I'm leaning towards waiting. Don't you always say Hartford is the only place to be for Christmas?"

Gaby looked at her lap. "I guess I would miss you."

Owen had mostly decided to stay. Gaby's simple sentence removed all doubts. "How was the tree lighting?" he asked, knowing that must be what had brought her down.

"Pretty much awful."

"Because of the rain?"

"Because people let the rain spoil it!" Gaby turned to Owen

and he could tell she was about to burst with the details. "First of all," she said, "Santa – who I'm sorry to say no longer deserves the title – didn't want to get the costume wet and the best thing he could think of was to wave at people from his car. There was no hot chocolate. I found Judy Smithburger and asked her what was up with that and she said they didn't think many people would want to drink it in the rain so it wasn't worth the effort to set up the stand. And she even admitted that now they had no idea what to do with the supplies they'd already bought. And the mayor flipped the switch early because he wanted to go home. He didn't even tell people he was going to do that so we didn't get a countdown going.

"I found a few people willing to sing and it fell apart on the second song. They acted like they didn't know the words to *Joy to the World*. Who doesn't know *Joy to the World*?"

Owen only shrugged. It felt best to let Gaby vent for a bit.

"When I got home," she continued more quietly, "I started trying to think about some past tree lightings. I thought I could cheer myself up with some happy memories. It only made me more upset though because I decided that my favorite one was actually another time that it rained."

"When was that?"

"It was our senior year of high school. I remember because I went with Derek Slawson and that's when I dated him. My little sisters tagged along. At first no one seemed to care that it was raining. Mr. Overmeyer had an umbrella and a big, clear poncho over his Santa suit. He joked that he'd have held off washing his reindeer if he'd known they were just going to get rained on. Told the joke over and over as new people arrived to hear it.

"We started the countdown and with every number more umbrellas got folded up to avoid blocking the view. People were reveling in the soggy mess by then and we started the caroling with *O Holy Night*. I think it was supposed to be ironic to sing about a beautiful night during one that was so dismal... but it wasn't. There was some sort of Christmas magic happening. We sang it at least three times and people were literally falling on their knees because we couldn't get any wetter. I think Seth might have started that. Do you remember that night?"

"It doesn't sound familiar," Owen said. "I must not have gone that year."

"I know Jimmy wasn't there anyway. Jess was looking for him. She had a big crush on him back then."

"Really?"

"Yeah, I'm guessing it's been long enough that she wouldn't care about me telling you." Gaby almost smiled and then she remembered the reason she was sulking. "I don't know why people couldn't try a little harder tonight to enjoy themselves."

"What would have made tonight better? Specifically. Maybe we can think up the perfect tree lighting."

"Hot chocolate for one. I wouldn't mind if a few drops of rain splashed into it. That would have just cooled it off so you could drink it faster."

"What else?"

"Um, Santa. He was parked like half a block away so some people probably didn't even know he was there. I'm sure there could have been a better way to keep the costume dry."

"Okay, now I have an idea. Do you have a pen?" Owen was ready to give Jill's project a try. He opened the packages of paper and cut strips – he'd remembered scissors but not a pen – from a sheet of each color. Gaby brought him a pen and handed it over with a curious expression. "This is what Jill suggested," Owen said. "A paper chain. We're going to use it to remake tonight's tree lighting."

Gaby leaned in enough to watch him write "rain-infused hot chocolate" on a red strip of paper and "more imaginative Santa" on a green one. He taped them with the words facing out to make the first two links and then looked at Gaby expectantly. "What else should have happened?"

"People remembered the words to basic Christmas songs."

Owen nodded and wrote "sing *Joy to the World*, all 4 verses."

"And *you* should have come," Gaby said. "We'd have had fun in the rain." She looked at him as though she believed his presence would have improved the whole evening. It made him want to kiss her but he knew that would be a wrong turn for the evening. He turned back to their project and concentrated on friendly thoughts. Gaby laughed when he wrote "Owen is tied up and dragged there."

"Now you add something," she said.

He grabbed a green strip but didn't write on it. "This is for you."

"No, really. If we had the perfect tree lighting, you'd want to come. What might entice you to come?"

"Um… cookies." He wrote "free Christmas cookies."

"Wait." Gaby took the pen from him and added "with tons of sprinkles."

She turned that into a link on the chain while Owen reclaimed the pen and wrote "live band to lead the singing."

"That would be fun," Gaby said. Then she filled about two dozen links with requests for her favorite Christmas songs.

Owen added a few songs as well and tried to slip in a link that said "mistletoe." When Gaby saw it her eyebrows went up slightly, then she blushed while she wrote "someone to meet under the mistletoe."

"That was kind of implied," Owen said. He didn't point out that she already said he should be there. He was afraid she'd realize he wasn't joking.

"Yeah, well, I don't need to list all the carols separately either. Where's the fun in a short chain?"

"Oh, I got one."

Gaby watched over his shoulder and read it out loud as he wrote. "'Forget to plug in the lights.' Owen! This is supposed to be a good tree lighting."

"That is good. Remember when that happened two years ago? It was funny and we got to do the countdown twice."

"Actually, you're right. It sort of prolonged the big moment." Gaby looked dreamy as she remembered the incident. Then she broke out in a huge grin. "Oh! I have the best idea yet. We get to hang up the ornaments!"

Owen didn't think being put to work would be an incentive to attend, but he still liked her idea. It helped with his birthday present dilemma. He was planning a present he knew she'd like when he realized Gaby had said something else for him to write. "What?" he asked.

"*The Holly and the Ivy*. I thought of another song."

"I don't think even you know the words to that one."

"That's another idea," Gaby said. "Pass out sheet music."

Owen wrote her idea and another of his own. She attached her link and then took his to read before adding the tape. "'Rain turns into snow.' That would be perfect. I don't think anyone has ever imagined a better evening."

And they weren't finished. Mostly due to Gaby's extensive knowledge of Christmas carols, they were able to make a chain that hung all the way around her living room.

When he got the last section taped up, Owen watched Gaby admire their work. "Do I get a surprise now?"

"Oh, yeah," she said as she bent to reach under her couch. She pulled out a red and green scarf. It looked as though most of the stripes were different widths. Owen appreciated the uniqueness but Gaby began to apologize for it as she handed the scarf to him. "I know it looks funny with different stripes. But I lost count of the rows on one of the early ones and then I thought if I made most of them different on purpose that would sort of cover... It would look like that was what I was going for."

He tried to wipe the smile from his face because he wasn't laughing at the gift, but at its location. "It's great. Really. But, um... why was it under the couch?"

Gaby's face conceded that could be considered a strange place to store a scarf. "I got in the habit of stuffing it under the couch when I wasn't working on it to make sure I didn't accidentally leave it in sight when you came over. Then I didn't really think about putting it anywhere else when it was done."

Owen put the scarf around his neck and threw one side over his shoulder. "It fits," he said.

"Of course it fits." She looked as though she was working to keep her eyes from rolling at him. "Now you need to wear it every day until December 28th."

"Why the 28th?"

"Well, ideally you'd wear a Christmas scarf until Epiphany, but I'm not counting on that."

"How about if I just wear it until, you know, it's not cold anymore?"

The sigh she began her answer with said she had little hope of Owen understanding much of anything... ever. "It's a Christmas scarf. If you wear it when it's not Christmas time, you diminish its Christmas power."

"What kind of Christmas power does it have?" Owen pretended to examine the scarf. "X-ray vision? Super speed? Stain resistance?"

Gaby was shaking her head, clearly not able to correct him because she was trying not to laugh.

"Is it electrical power? Or maybe it throws flames? That would be cool."

"All right," Gaby said. "Thanks for coming over but I think it's time for you to leave."

Owen nodded and began moving towards her door. "I'll try to respect the power of the Christmas scarf, as soon as I figure out what it does."

"Goodnight, Owen."

He waved with the end of the scarf and Gaby had a big smile when she closed the door behind him, her irritation over the disappointing tree lighting completely forgotten. Owen returned to his side of the building knowing that he owed Jill an apology for thinking she was anything less than a genius.

Chapter 8

"Gabrielle, you're never going to guess what Kevin's giving me for Christmas."

Gaby looked up at Krista. "Do *you* know what he's getting you?"

"Of course."

"But Christmas is two and a half weeks away. It's not going to be a surprise?"

Krista gave a condescending smile. "If I let him surprise me, I wouldn't get what I want."

"So you picked out your own gift?"

"Yeah. Now guess what it is."

This was not a game that Gaby wanted to play. She suspected that Krista would mock any incorrect guesses. "I don't think I'll be very good at guessing," she said. "Can you tell me what it is?"

"Sometimes you're not any fun. But anyway, he's giving me a necklace with my birthstone. It's very nice and we had it wrapped at the store so it's already under the tree. You know we ended up putting up his stupid artificial tree because he refused to get a real one and I figured a fake tree was better than nothing."

"I'd love a real tree but they cost more. I usually let myself spend about the amount of a real tree on extra decorations each year."

Krista made a face as though she was suddenly nauseated. "You're one of those people who buys Christmas stuff in January for the next year, aren't you?"

"Sure. What's wrong with buying stuff on sale?"

"Nothing in general. But I cannot look at Christmas stuff in January."

"More for me," Gaby said. A masculine laugh came from behind her. She turned to see Jared standing on the other side of the counter. "Hi."

"Your cookies are delicious, Gaby," he said.

61

"Thanks. I'm happy you like them."

"I meant to wait until after lunch but they were sitting right in front of me and I couldn't resist."

"I'm sorry I tempted you."

Jared's eyes crinkled when he smiled. "No, you're not."

"I could be sorry."

"I have something for you." He slid a folded piece of paper across the counter. He waited until her hand was on it before he pulled his away.

"What's this?" she asked.

"Read it."

Gaby opened the note, furtively making sure that Krista stayed on her side of the divider. It said "Can you come back from lunch a few minutes early and meet me out back?"

Gaby nodded. "Yes, I can."

"Good." Jared winked at Krista and then said, "See you later," to Gaby. Gaby shredded the paper as he walked away.

"Gabrielle, what is going on with you two?"

Gaby shrugged innocently.

"Are you going out with him?"

"I, um… I don't think I want to talk about that right now."

"But I tell you about Kevin all the time."

"Yes," Gaby said. "You tell me. I don't ask."

Krista clammed up and appeared offended that Gaby didn't want to share details of her personal life. Those details were making Gaby very uncomfortable already. She didn't know what Jared wanted to talk about, but she did know that she'd barely thought about him all weekend. If he asked her out again she'd have to turn him down and that would not be fun.

Even less fun was the turmoil she was facing over Owen. Between the cookie making and the tree lighting fantasy, he'd given her one of the most amazing weekends of her life. He'd also made it impossible for her to continue pretending she wasn't falling for him. That wasn't supposed to happen. They were supposed to stay friends. If he found out and didn't feel the same way, then things would get weird and she'd lose having him in her life. Irrational or not, she was angry with Owen for making her face those feelings.

She had no idea what to do and the best plan she had so far was to avoid him for a few days to see if that helped.

Jared she could not avoid. They'd only had one date though so she hoped whatever scene was waiting for her after lunch wouldn't be overly awkward. He was standing by the back door when she arrived.

"Hi, Jared."

"Hi. Thanks for meeting me."

Gaby nodded, then waited for Jared to say why he wanted to talk to her.

"Thanks for the cookies," he said.

"You already thanked me."

"Yeah, um…" Jared shifted a little. "Friday I sort of got the impression that you wouldn't be interested in going out with me again. Was I wrong?"

Gaby bit her lip. "I'm sorry but no. Probably not. Or maybe but—"

Jared looked relieved as he cut her off. "No, you don't have to… I mean I'm not flattered that you're not interested but…" He stopped and sighed. "I don't know if I owe you an apology or just an explanation but I know I came on kind of strong at first and I think I should tell you the truth."

"Um, I don't think you really owe me anything."

"I just want you to know that I'm not backing off because of you. The truth is… and I know you'll keep this to yourself… I'm recently divorced. Some people might say the ink's barely dry. I realized a little too late that I'm not ready to try again."

"Oh, I'm really sorry about that."

"But there's no hard feelings between us?"

Gaby shook her head emphatically. "In fact, I wouldn't mind at all if you wanted to keep popping up front to see me."

"Very good. I enjoy the look on Krista's face when I surprise you."

"You are good at that."

"Thanks," Jared said. "So if I tease Krista by flirting with you, we'll both know that's all it is and be okay with that?"

"Yes."

Jared waved his ID in front of the door lock and then opened the door. "After you then," he said.

Gaby smiled as she walked in first. Krista returned from lunch a minute later. She had evidently finished sulking over Gaby's need

63

for privacy (or forgot about it) because she kept up her usual stream of conversation during all the slow times in the afternoon and for the next two days as well.

By Thursday, she had even returned to her attempts to get Gaby to share.

"Gabrielle, he's been stopping by to talk to you every day. He obviously likes you."

"I'm a nice person. Why wouldn't he?"

"That's not what I mean. Has Jared asked you out yet?"

"I know you listen. Have you heard him ask me out?"

Krista flipped her hair back impatiently and said, "I don't know why you have to be so stubborn."

Gaby tried to change the subject. "Did you talk Kevin into coming to the office party?"

"No. He's terrible." She lowered her voice in an attempt to imitate him. "You keep saying it's going to be the most boring thing ever. Why would I want to go?" Krista rolled her eyes and resumed her natural tone. "I said it would be boring if he didn't come. He doesn't understand that having a boyfriend means I'm supposed to have a date for this kind of thing. Gabrielle, what about you? Are you going to be alone tomorrow?"

Gaby shook her head. "Nope. A lot of my coworkers will be there."

"That's not funny."

"I thought it was sort of funny."

Gaby jumped at the sound of Jared's voice and then laughed. He was good at sneaking up on her but that was the first time she'd actually jumped.

He noticed. "Gotcha," he said with a smile.

"Yes, you did. Now what do you want?"

"Believe it or not, I'm actually in line."

"In line?"

Jared glanced at Krista and then returned his attention to Gaby. "You ladies do handle financial transactions up here, right?"

"Oh, you're pretending to be a customer?" Gaby said.

"I *am* a customer."

"All right." She adopted a fake serious demeanor. "What can I do for you today, Mr. Greener?"

He placed a five-dollar bill on the counter. "I would like change for the drink machine, please."

****

Friday was different. Or rather, Krista was different on Friday. She came in looking as though she had something on her mind, which was not unusual. The difference was that she didn't seem to want to say whatever it was. The morning passed more quietly than usual and without Krista distracting her after lunch, Gaby actually saw Jared slip out of his office and approach the counter.

"Afternoon, ladies," he said.

Krista nodded stiffly at him. Gaby acknowledged his presence a bit more warmly. "What brings you out of your office on this fine Friday?" she asked.

"Maybe I thought the view was better out here." He locked eyes on Gaby and she did not look away. She actually enjoyed his visits more since they decided that flirting would be the extent of their relationship. She could simply relax and enjoy it.

She said, "Maybe you just improved the view from this side of the counter."

He laughed. "Anything else I can do to brighten your day?"

"Hmm... I'll have to think about that. What are you offering?"

Jared reached into the inner pocket of his suit coat and pulled out about two feet of silver garland. "How about this?" he asked, and he proceeded to tie it to the chain holding a pen to her counter.

"Did you steal that from the break room?"

He shook his head. "As far as you know I brought that from home especially for you."

"How sweet."

"Not entirely," he said. "It might be a bribe."

"You're trying to bribe me with a piece of tinsel?"

"It's Christmas cheer. My understanding is that's a valuable commodity for you."

Gaby glanced at Krista, who was doing a better job of pretending not to eavesdrop than usual. "Okay," Gaby said, "let's hear what you want in exchange."

He leaned across the counter and lowered his voice slightly. "I decided to make an appearance at the party tonight and someone has threatened to keep me company. I hoped I could talk you into staying close enough to run interference. I won't stay long."

Gaby nodded her understanding. He wanted her to shield him from another woman's advances. She had done that for Owen once. "I'll do what I can," she said. "But only because you're paying me." She brushed the fluffy garland with her fingertips.

Jared stepped back and smiled at her and at Krista. "Until tonight then, both of you."

Gaby watched him return to his office. Even without sparks, it really was a nice view. If there were many single women at the other bank branches, she might have her work cut out for her.

"Gabrielle, I..."

Gaby looked at Krista. That was the third time she had started to talk and then stopped. It was getting annoying.

"Gabrielle, I... well, that sort of almost sounded like Jared was asking you out."

"I guess it did sound *sort of* and *almost* like asking me out. But he wasn't."

"It's just that... I saw something." Krista whispered the last part.

Gaby lowered her voice as well, even though there was no one else around. "What did you see?"

"This morning, when I came in, Jared was in his office and... he was playing with something on his desk." Krista's eyes darted around and then landed back on Gaby. "It looked like a wedding ring and he put it in his pocket."

"Oh..." Gaby felt a flood of sympathy for Jared. If he was still carrying around a wedding ring, then he was definitely not ready to date. She also felt curiosity that she worked to squash. What he had already told her was in confidence. This was none of her business and it was none of Krista's business either. "Are you sure it was a wedding ring?" she asked Krista. "Maybe it was something else or maybe it wasn't his?"

"I think I know what a wedding ring looks like and why would a guy have some other guy's ring?"

Gaby shrugged. "I don't know."

Krista studied her for a moment. "I think there's something you're not telling me."

"I just don't think you should jump to any conclusions," Gaby

66

said, trying to end the conversation before she gave away that she knew anything.

"Do you..." Krista stopped and looked towards the front door as it opened to let in a customer.

Gaby looked that way as well and her stomach did a complete backflip at the sight of the guy with blonde hair and a red-and-green-striped scarf. She hadn't seen Owen all week and her plan did not appear to be working. She smiled brightly at him as he approached her counter. "What are you doing here?" she asked.

"Nice," he answered. "Is that how you greet all your customers?"

"Of course not. But I happen to know you're an ATM kind of guy. What brings you inside?"

"I'm doing a favor for a coworker. Apparently the grandkids are getting cash for Christmas. She wants some of those envelopes you guys have with a hole for the president's face."

"Sure." Gaby opened a drawer and pulled out an envelope in each hand. She held them up and asked, "Does she want 'Happy Holidays' or 'Seasons Greetings'?"

Owen appeared unsure. "I don't think she knew there was a choice."

"How many?" Gaby asked.

"Eight."

"Okay. I'll give you eight 'Seasons Greetings' because those are prettier and I'll throw in a 'Happy Holidays' so she can send you back if you made the wrong choice."

"If *I* made the wrong choice?"

Gaby smiled at him while she counted out the envelopes.

He took them and said, "I'm only taking credit if it's the right choice."

"I can live with that."

"Have you finished those sappy movies yet?"

"I think I'm caught up." Gaby had used wanting to watch some Christmas romances as an excuse not to get together twice that week. "Bank thing tonight though. Do you want to make me dinner tomorrow?"

He cocked his head to the side. "Are you inviting yourself over?"

"Would you rather come to my place and order pizza?"

67

"I can probably think of something to make," he said as he tapped the sides of the envelopes against the counter. "I assume you've been eating frozen dinners all week."

"Maybe."

"Well, I better run. Thanks for these." Owen waved the envelopes in the air as he turned from the counter.

"See you tomorrow, Owen," she called after him.

"Gabrielle, did you just call that guy Owen?"

"I did, as a matter of fact." She turned to Krista. "That's his name."

"That's not... Is that the same Owen who lives next door to you?"

"Yeah, why?"

Krista gaped at her. "I guess when you said you were friends with your neighbor I assumed he was either really old or really ugly and that guy," she pointed at the door Owen had left through, "was neither."

Gaby shrugged. "That doesn't mean I can't be his friend." She began fiddling with some paperwork, hoping Krista would think she meant that as nonchalantly as it sounded. But she couldn't stop thinking how good Owen looked wearing the scarf she'd made for him. He'd always been an attractive guy. Why was she suddenly noticing it every time she saw him? Even as she asked herself the question though, Gaby knew it wasn't all that sudden. She'd been fighting it for a long time because she didn't like change.

"Gabrielle, I have to ask. Is that why everything is hush hush between you and Jared?"

Gaby didn't even look up. "I'm sorry," she said, "but it's really none of your business." Her thoughts were consumed with Owen and she was completely unaware that Krista had gone back to talking about the wedding ring.

****

Gaby had been to three other bank holiday parties. The fourth was very similar. They reserved the same convention space at a hotel in Port Harris. The buffet was catered by the same company. They served the same delicious meatballs and the same perfectly steamed broccoli. And they ruined the cheesecake again, too.

68

Gaby didn't understand how professional cooks could ruin cheesecake, but it had a bizarre gritty texture. Her first bite was one of the few times in recent memory she'd been hoping against consistency.

Each round table in the room had eight chairs. Jared sat next to Gaby while they ate. Everyone else at the table worked at one of the other three branches of the Hartford Bank, or was a spouse to one of those employees. The conversation began with introductions and small talk and was quickly dominated by the last couple to sit down. They were clear extroverts and held court over the table for the duration of the meal.

There was music and a dance floor that were oddly incompatible. Gaby had no intention of dancing in front of coworkers anyway. Jared left almost as soon as he was done eating and Gaby mingled for no more than five minutes. She got the weird feeling that Krista was avoiding her. She seemed to spend a lot of time looking in Gaby's direction without coming over to say hello. Gaby was bored of the event and she drove home.

It was only around 9 pm when she arrived in Hartford so she took a slight detour to admire the downtown decorations and the large tree at the park. There were a few brightly lit houses as well, all of them beautiful and beautifully familiar.

Gaby was happy to see that Owen also had his lights on. He'd said when she first hung the string for him that he'd probably forget to plug them in all the time but that hadn't been a problem. She considered knocking on his door since it was kind of early for a Friday. She went straight to her own side instead. They already had plans to see each other on Saturday. It was probably better if she spent the rest of the evening trying not to think about him.

That plan, however, was doomed to failure. Her living room was surrounded by a red, green and white reminder of her thoughtful neighbor. He'd gone out of his way to find a Christmas project because Gaby liked Christmasy things. Then he'd used it to cheer her up when she was disappointed that something he thought was boring turned out to actually be boring. And Gaby had barely realized how sweet it was because that was just the kind of friend Owen was, even before they were friends. He could have laughed when she sought protection from a very fragile eight-legged critter.

The leftover construction paper was still sitting in her living room. She picked it up and began to cut links for a new chain. She planned to use green links for each nice thing Owen had done for her and red links for each time she had returned the favor. The green links were easy. She started with one for the other chain. She added one for the time he carried her parents' old chair up the stairs for her and one for the time he'd driven halfway to the city to change a tire. He'd never done it before either and stood by the side of the road reading instructions on his phone while she watched. He helped her list all of Mason's negative qualities when he wanted to "find a more exciting relationship." Owen had gone with her to her grandmother's funeral. And the last time he washed his car, he'd done hers just because he already had the bucket handy.

Gaby let herself add one red link to represent cookies and sat looking at the disparity. She hadn't added green links for all the times Owen had made her dinner. She needed to stop letting her mind go other places with him and start counting herself lucky to even be his friend.

She picked up her phone and texted Owen: Change of plan. I'm cooking tomorrow.

Owen: Really!? What are you making?

Gaby: I don't know yet.

Owen: Good plan.

She could picture the sarcasm on his face as he typed that reply. It didn't matter. She was going to the Market in the morning and could surely find something to make. She picked up a red strip of paper and made a link for the dinner she hadn't made yet. Then she worked on green links until she wanted to get ready for bed, alternating between feeling mushy about the nice things Owen did and feeling bad that she didn't deserve them.

Chapter 9

Gaby got a much slower start that Saturday than the previous one when she'd been looking forward to making cookies. She squinted against the bright sun as she locked her door behind her. Something felt wrong as she turned and pulled her gloves out of her pockets. There were tiny colored bits scattered on her porch that she could not immediately identify. As she examined the scene, she saw that it was colored glass from her Christmas lights. At least half of the bulbs were broken.

She pulled out her phone. Owen was always the first person who came to mind. She texted: Are you up? Did you hear anything weird last night?

Owen didn't need to answer the first question when he replied but he sent: Yes. No. Why?

Gaby: I'm outside. My lights are broken.

Owen opened his front door pulling a sweatshirt over his T-shirt and pajama pants. "What's going on?" he asked.

"I don't know but stay there. There's glass."

Owen was barefoot. He took a few careful steps onto the porch. "Are they all broken?"

Gaby shook her head. "No, but enough that I don't think it was weather or, well, accidental."

Owen looked over the lights on his side of the building. "Mine are intact."

"I know," Gaby said, "that kind of makes this seem… aimed at me."

"You think it was personal?"

"Maybe. I mean, this is Hartford. Everyone knows I live here."

"I think you should call the police."

"No. Don't. I don't want to make it a bigger deal. And how much will it cost me to replace a couple strings of lights? That's not worth anyone's time."

"I'm going to tell Jimmy."

71

Gaby tried to protest. "Don't bother him. Really. It's not worth it."

"Don't worry, it won't be anything official. But if he or someone else can keep an eye out... I'll feel better."

There was concern on Owen's face and she began to wish she'd tried to replace the lights before he noticed. "Relax, Owen," she said. "I'm sure I'm not in danger from someone who breaks Christmas lights in the middle of the night. I'm offended on behalf of the holiday and a little curious about the motivation, but not scared at all. I'll just go to the city after lunch and get new lights."

"I'm still going to call Jimmy. And it's too cold to stand out here arguing about it." He waved to Gaby as he stepped backwards and closed his door.

Owen was right about the cold anyway. Gaby decided to leave the damaged lights alone until she had replacements. Hopefully, it would be a few degrees warmer by then. She ran down the stairs and tried to get some heat going in her car. The air from the vents was only beginning to feel warm when she arrived at the Market. Visitors might feel put off by the faded exterior or even alarmed by the old-fashioned doors that swung out automatically. But Gaby was welcomed by the familiar sights and sounds.

She picked up a few standard items from the freezers and some fresh fruit and dry cereal. Now she only needed something to cook for dinner. After a bit of aimless wandering, she called her mother.

"Hi, Gaby. What is my favorite oldest daughter up to this morning?"

"Mom, I have a question. How do you make chicken?" Gaby was staring at a case filled with various cuts of poultry. She usually liked chicken.

"You'll have to be more specific," her mom said.

"Chicken. You know, the meat that comes from the bird of the same name."

Penny Bryant laughed through the phone. "Honey, there are about a million different ways to make chicken. What are you looking for?"

"I don't know. Something easy and without any skin or bones to deal with." She grabbed something cold from the shelf. "This one says boneless breasts. How do I cook that?"

"That depends. What are you making with it? Do you want it

to be plain or spicy or cheesy or in a sauce or..."

Gaby put the package back down before she interrupted. "Mom, wait... That's going to be too complicated. We need to do this a different way."

"What way?"

"Hang on." Gaby thought for a moment about some of the meals her mom made that Owen might like. "What about that cheeseburger pie you make sometimes? Is that easy?"

"Very."

"Okay. Give me a minute to get some paper and then tell me what I need." Gaby fished around in her purse and then copied the recipe as her mom explained it. She was fairly sure she could handle it. And she bought a can of green beans to warm up and add some color to the plates.

When she returned home, her light strings had been removed and the glass swept up. Owen. She hadn't asked him to do that. Why did he have to be so sweet all the time? It almost felt as though he was trying to remind her that he could be the perfect guy for her when she was trying very hard not to think about him like that.

She put away her groceries and ate a banana because it was after noon and she wanted to get to the city and back soon. She stopped at three stores and the cheap multi-colored lights were sold out at all of them. It wasn't that she had anything against the other choices, it was that people in town had seen her other lights. She wanted to get the same kind to make it less obvious that something had happened. She ended up buying some strings of green lights and some of red and hoping that people would assume the others had simply burned out.

Owen's car was gone when she got home. She quickly hung up her new lights before he could show up and be helpful again. Then she sent him a text that said: Come over around 5 to watch the magic happen.

Gaby opened her door to him at exactly 5 pm. He walked in with his hands behind his back.

"What do you have?" Gaby asked.

Owen took a deep breath before he pulled Gaby's big red bow from behind his back. "I tried to like this, really. But these dangly parts keep getting caught in the door every time I open the freezer."

"And how often do you open your freezer?"

"Often enough for it to be annoying."

Gaby took the bow out of Owen's hand. "Why didn't you just put it somewhere else?"

"I did. I put it in your hands." He smirked at her.

She felt warm and tossed the bow over the back of her couch in an attempt to act casually. "You didn't try very hard to like it."

Owen followed the bow with his eyes and noticed her new paper chain on the floor. "You're working on a new chain?"

"Sort of."

Owen looked amused. "That looks like a chain. How is it *sort of* a chain?"

"It was part of a... project."

"A making a paper chain project?"

"No. It was more like a..." Gaby was struggling for the words she wanted. "Like a visual representation of something else."

"Of what?"

"Well, I don't think I want to tell you that."

"Why is it almost all green?"

"That's kind of...part of..."

"Part of what you don't want to tell me."

Gaby nodded.

Owen did not look offended. He still looked amused. "All right," he said. "So what are you making me tonight? Is that also a secret?"

Gaby smiled. "Yes, that can be a secret, too."

"Will I know what it is when I eat it?"

"The only thing that matters is that you will know you love it. But I'm not going to try to hide the ingredients."

Owen followed her into the kitchen. "Ingredients?" he said. "That sounds serious."

"It's not like I've *never* cooked before."

"Wait. You have? Was I there?"

Owen was only teasing and she knew it. She'd usually enjoy it. But the fact that it had been at least six months since she'd made any attempt to make dinner for them was weighing on her. She ignored the comment and reached into a lower cabinet for a skillet.

"Can I help?" Owen asked.

"No." It was her turn and if he did half the work it wouldn't count. Her answer came out more forceful than she intended though. "I mean, you don't know what I'm making."

Owen tried to hang back a bit while Gaby turned on the stove and pulled some ground beef from her refrigerator. It felt as though something was bothering her and he didn't know what it was. Or if it was his imagination. He still couldn't figure out whether or not she had intentionally blown him off during the week. While it was true that she liked cheesy Christmas romances and he did not, they still felt like an excuse not to get together. Previous years she'd at least asked, however jokingly, if he wanted to join her. She had even once managed to trick him into watching one.

Gaby was focused on browning the meat. Her right hand worked a heavy spoon across the pan while her left arm rested at her side. Owen wanted to take that free hand in both of his and feel how soft her skin was. He wanted to step closer and breathe in the vanilla scent of her hair. Maybe even brush some of it aside to kiss the back of her neck. He couldn't do any of that and she had no idea how she tortured him just by standing there.

He walked the few steps back to the living room to clear his head and picked up that red bow as a reason for the sudden movement. He carried it back to the kitchen and began tying it to Gaby's freezer. "I think maybe you should try to like this bow for a while," he said to break the silence.

Gaby seemed relieved. It was unusual for them to have awkward silence. "It's Christmasy," she said. "How could I not like it?"

"Trust me," he said. "About the fourth time this thing gets caught in the door, you're going to want to hurl it across the room."

"I doubt that. This room could use a little festivity."

Owen looked around the room. Gaby's tree and lights had come out on the day after Thanksgiving. The rest appeared gradually so that there was now a Merry Christmas banner on one wall, poinsettia window clingys over the sink, a red-and-green plaid cushion tied to each of the two kitchen chairs, bows or glitter balls tied to each of the cabinet handles, and where they had rolled out cookies there was a large porcelain nativity scene. "A little festivity?

I'm trying to remember if you have any decorations I haven't seen yet this year."

"I have one more box at my parents' house. I'll get it tomorrow and I'll find something in it for your place."

Owen let out a short laugh and said, "Is that a threat?"

Gaby pulled the pan off the burner and set it aside. She turned around to face him and was biting the side of her lower lip. "Does it really feel like I'm threatening you?"

It should have been obvious that he was only teasing. He stopped smiling. "Gaby, what's wrong?"

"Nothing."

"Really nothing or nothing you want to talk about?"

"Really nothing." She turned back to the counter and poured some biscuit mix into a bowl.

Owen didn't believe that there was nothing bothering her but after a few quiet moments he tried a different subject. "So," he started, "next Saturday is your birthday."

"Yeah, believe it or not, I already knew that."

"I was thinking a little about how we should celebrate."

"Really?" Gaby seemed a bit confused by the meal preparation. She pulled a piece of paper from her pocket and nodded as she stuffed it back. Then she grabbed some mustard from her refrigerator.

"Yes, really," Owen said. "I think you liked the dinner and Christmas tree cake last year, right?"

She nodded and he saw a slight smile.

"And I know you like traditions."

She nodded again.

"But you're going to be at your parents house most of the day since your sisters are coming home."

"Oh, that's right."

"I thought maybe you could come over for dinner on Friday and again Saturday morning so we could do dinner but you could still get your present on your birthday."

"Dinner *and* a present? Owen, that's too much."

"The present isn't a big deal," he said. He didn't understand why she looked worried. Was it because he wanted to see her two days in a row? Was it *not* his imagination that she was trying to cut back their time together? Had he somehow given her a hint of his

76

true feelings for her? The thought that she might now be uncomfortable around him was not a welcome one. It entered his mind anyway.

She turned abruptly back to face him and said, "And why did you clean up my broken lights?"

"What?"

"It was you, wasn't it?"

"Yeah," he said slowly. Why did it sound like she was accusing him of a crime? "I didn't want you to cut yourself."

"Did *you?*"

"Did I what?"

"Did you cut yourself?" she asked.

Owen was becoming more unsure with each answer. He was beginning to think he was wrong about why Gaby was upset but was doubtful he'd prefer the real reason. "No," he said, "I was careful."

"I could have been careful."

"Yes. I know you would have but... I was trying to be nice."

"I know that." Gaby tore open a package of shredded cheese with more gusto than necessary and then sighed as she put it on the counter with a defeated look on her face. "It's just," she said. "It's just that... you made me have to add another link."

Owen took a small step closer to her. "Gaby, please tell me what you're talking about."

She sighed again and gestured to her living room. "That's what the chain was all about."

"The one on the floor in there?"

"Yes."

He walked quickly to the next room and brought the paper chain back. "There's nothing written on the links."

"I was keeping track in my head."

"Of what?"

Gaby hesitated and began to turn red. She looked at the floor. "I put a green link whenever I thought of something you've done for me and a red link for the other way around."

"What are the two red links for?"

"Cookies and this dinner that I might someday get into the oven."

"And the green ones?"

77

"All kinds of things?"

"Like what?"

"A lot of them are also for dinners."

Owen put the paper on the kitchen table and tipped his head slightly to one side. "Let me get this straight. I get a link for each dinner and you only get one for cookies even though you make me cookies like once a month?"

Gaby kept her mouth shut and kept looking at the floor.

"And what about the time you pretended to be my date at that office thing?" he continued. "And you let me do laundry over here both times my washing machine was broken and you know what? I'm not going to list anything else. I don't know what kind of funk you let yourself get into but you don't keep score in a friendship." He tore off all the links except for one each of red and green and held those two in front of Gaby.

She said, "Can I hug you?"

That was an unexpected request but one he would never refuse. He opened his arms and she jumped against him. "What's really bothering you?" he whispered to the top of her head and felt it shake in response. It was unlike Gaby to appear emotionally fragile. He simply kept holding her because he didn't know what else to do.

Gaby didn't want the hug to end. She felt Owen's hand come up and lightly stroke the back of her hair. She suddenly felt like a child for trying to count good deeds. Her emotions were just a mess where Owen was concerned. Leaning against him, she felt more than comfort and more than a simple attraction. She had to admit she was completely head over heels for this guy who had just said you couldn't keep score in a *friendship*. The word hit her like ice and she jumped backwards. "I need to finish this or we'll never get to eat," she said.

Owen quietly watched her get their dinner into the oven. She turned to face him but couldn't think of anything to say, couldn't think of how to get past that ridiculous chain on her kitchen table. Finally, Owen picked it up. "Well," he said, "if we *were* going to do this... we'd need to take off links for the not-so-nice times." The look on his face suggested he was trying to lighten the mood.

"What do you mean?" Gaby asked.

"If I get a link for every time I made dinner, we also need to take one off for that time I said I was going to cook and we ended up splitting a bag of chips." Owen tore off a green link and then went after the only other red one. "And you don't get to keep this one because of the time you signed me up to ride on a Yam Fest float without asking me first."

Gaby laughed at the memory. They'd had a lot of fun on that float once Owen got over being annoyed with her. She pointed at the now all-green chain. "At least now I don't have anything left to lose. But you can take off a green one for each of the perfectly good Christmas decorations you've returned this year."

Owen held a link but did not tear it. "I had perfectly good reasons for returning all of them."

"No, you didn't. And while you're at it, you can take off a link for the time you hid all the vowels."

"Come on," he said, "that was funny." He tore off links at the same time.

"It was not! I traded in my letters three times before I figured out you were cheating."

"I wasn't cheating. I was playing a trick."

"And it wasn't funny," Gaby insisted. It was obvious how hard she was working not to laugh.

Owen held up a torn piece of green paper as though he was taunting her with it.

Gaby snatched it from his hand and said, "And there was the time you stole my phone."

"Oh, you're reaching now. You know I didn't steal it. You're the one who left it at my place."

"But you laughed when I said I lost it and it was in your pocket!"

"Only so I could give it back to you. And it still pales in comparison to the Yam Fest incident."

"Now it's an incident? Let's not forget *why* I signed you up for that float. You totally deserved it after the popcorn thing."

A smile showed up on Owen's face and he couldn't squelch it before it gave away how much he did not feel guilty about the popcorn thing. "How many Cub Scouts did you end up buying from again?"

"Eleven. And most of them came back this year."

"Apparently, I wasn't wrong when I told them you were a sucker."

"That's not the point," Gaby said with a sigh. "But they are so cute in those uniforms and when they act all nervous and say please and ma'am and stuff, it's hard to say no."

"It doesn't work on everyone."

"Had a lot of doors slammed in your face back in the day?"

"That implies people even opened the doors to begin with."

"That's harsh," she said. Gaby had noticed that Owen casually stuffed the remains of her chain into a trash can while they were talking. She wished it would be as easy to remove her uncomfortable feelings for Owen but she did manage to push them aside for another evening.

Chapter 10

Owen was still puzzling over Gaby's odd behavior while he was at church the next day. A preachy voice in his head kept telling him to pay attention and stop trying to sneak looks at Gaby to see if she seemed distracted. He knew there was something going on with her and that she didn't want to talk about it. There were a lot of reasons she might not want to tell him about something but he couldn't help fixating on the possibility that it had something to do with him. Was there a chance she was confused about their relationship? And could that confusion end with a change, a really good change?

As they were leaving, Owen's mom gave him a very preachy look, one he hadn't seen in a few years. She said, "You could just ask her."

He tried to look as though he didn't know what she was talking about. When that didn't appear to work, he said, "It's not that simple."

She replied with one of those Mom looks that meant something like, "You're wrong but I'm going to let you figure out that you're wrong."

Jimmy was even more irritating. As soon as the brothers were alone on the porch he said, "So I gather you haven't convinced her you're a guy yet."

"That's really not the problem and it's not funny either."

"You could ask her out. You know, not make any declaration, just say you realized that you're a guy and she's— "

Owen gave his brother a gentle shove. "I told you that wasn't funny. And did you tell Mom?"

"Please. No one had to tell Mom anything. She likes Gaby and she's friends with her mom. They've probably been plotting to get you two together longer than you have."

Owen only grunted a response. It was true that their mom had dropped hints before about Gaby being "a nice girl."

Jimmy got suddenly serious and turned to his brother, "Look, man, I gotta tell you something that you're not going to like."

"Yeah?"

"Well, there's been no luck finding out anything about *who* broke Gaby's lights, but I might know *why*."

"You mean it was personal?"

"Maybe."

"What have you heard?"

"You know how she went out with that guy from the city who works at the bank?

Owen nodded. He didn't need to be reminded about that.

"Well, people are saying that he's married. And that Gaby is still seeing him even though she knows he's married."

"What!? Gaby would never—"

Jimmy held up his hands. "Don't shoot the messenger, okay? You know I don't believe it."

"How can anyone?"

"I'm sure it will blow over. People just get excited when they hear something and they'll realize it's ridiculous soon enough."

Owen sat on the steps shaking his head. He liked this new puzzle even less. There was usually a grain of truth to start a rumor like this. Was this guy – Gaby had called him Jared – was he actually married? Gaby would not have gone out with him if she knew, but maybe she found out later? That didn't make sense. She'd said she thought they were going to be friends. She would not have any such thoughts for a married guy who asked her out. Perhaps it was the other part that was true, the part about her still seeing him. That could be the reason for her weird behavior and the reason she'd avoided Owen during the week.

Gaby did not see Owen the rest of that Sunday. But she texted him late in the evening and they had the following exchange:

Gaby: Your mom said she caught you daydreaming in church. Shame on you.

Owen: I was not. And when did you talk to my mom?

Gaby: When she called me.

Owen: When did she call you?

Gaby: Today.

Owen: OK WHY did she call you?

Gaby: So we could talk about you.

Owen: What!?

Gaby: Not really. She wanted one of my cookie recipes.

Owen: You're not funny.

Gaby: Of course I am. That's why you love me.

Owen: I only love you for your cookies.

Gaby: Goodnight, Owen.

Owen: Goodnight.

Gaby watched the words fade as her phone went dark. She was humming Christmas carols as she got ready for bed and still happily thinking about the holiday as she tucked herself in. Owen's mom had expressed concern about him spending the day alone since the rest of his family was headed out of town. Gaby had assured her that there was no way she'd let him get out of celebrating with her. The only problem was that she hadn't decided on a present for Owen. She lay awake a long time trying to think of one, so long that her alarm felt particularly shrill in the morning.

Gaby jumped out of bed in a panic when she realized how many times she'd hit snooze. She rushed through her morning routine and managed to reach the front door at the appropriate time. She stepped outside and froze as she realized she was standing in a pile of something red. The wreath on her front door was made of red yarn. It was big and bright and very fluffy. Gaby had made it herself a few years earlier while sitting with her grandmother. It had taken several visits to the hospice to complete. She turned slowly to see what was left of it.

A scissor-wielding attacker had shredded one side of the wreath so that it was no longer anything like a circle. Gaby blinked hard and fast. As much as she loved decorations, she was not going to let herself cry over one. And especially not if it meant showing up for work with a blotchy face. She took the wreath off the door and tossed it on the floor just inside her apartment. She scooped up most of the fallen yarn and dropped it into the center of the wreath.

It already felt like a hectic morning. The two waiting customers added to the feeling and they entered as soon as the door was unlocked, the one on Gaby's side with a whole list of transactions. Krista was her usual talkative self, sharing stories of the ways Kevin had annoyed her over the weekend and showing off a new manicure. Gaby was more relieved than usual to go home for lunch and sit by herself for a few minutes.

She ate pretzels and stared at her battered wreath on the floor. The damage bothered her less than the fact that someone somewhere apparently felt she deserved it. Why? Had she offended someone? She couldn't think how.

No one could ruin Christmas for Gaby Bryant though. She would not let that happen. She put down her oh-so-healthy lunch and picked up the wreath. If she removed the rest of the yarn, she could reuse the foam circle underneath to make a new wreath. By the time she got back to work, she was almost looking forward to her new Christmas project.

"Gabrielle, I went to The Sandwich Shoppe for lunch and I got roast beef instead of turkey for a change."

"Yeah? Was it good?"

Krista looked thoughtful for a moment before answering. "Yes. I did like it."

Gaby nodded and caught sight of Jared out of the corner of her eye. She pointed at him. "I see you this time."

He rested his arm on the counter as he arrived. "So I guess we both got off easy at the party, huh?"

"I don't know who you were worried about, but I never noticed you needing help."

"I think Mr. and Mrs. Blowhard kept her at bay," he said. "All you had to do was occupy the chair."

"You know, I think I actually did that very well."

Jared smiled. "You fill a chair nicely. I'd say it was money well spent."

Gaby flicked at the tinsel still tied to her station and smiled as well.

"How was the rest of your weekend?"

Gaby shrugged. "Nothing special but not bad. Did you get your tree up?" Jared had mentioned at the party that his Christmas tree was still in its box.

He shook his head. "I might not bother."

"I don't understand people who think Christmas is a bother," Gaby said with an exaggerated sigh.

"There are things we don't understand about you either."

"Fair enough."

84

The front door opened and Jared greeted the customer before heading back to his office. When the front was empty again, Krista said, "Gabrielle, I'm surprised at you."

"Why are you surprised?"

"I know it's not really any of my business, but I thought you were all churchy and pious."

Ouch. Krista said churchy and pious as though they were negative qualities and yet still sounded disappointed to find that Gaby was neither. "Krista," Gaby said reluctantly, "what are you talking about?"

"You and Jared of course."

"Wait. Me and Jared what?"

Krista's eyebrows nearly disappeared into her hairline. "We all saw you guys leaving early on Friday."

"You're outraged that we got bored with a company event?"

"Let's just say you didn't fool anyone by giving him a head start."

"You think I went out with him afterwards?"

"Didn't you?"

"As a matter of fact, I did not," Gaby said. "But I don't understand why it would matter to you if I had."

"I think it would matter to his *wife*."

"His..." Gaby let her mouth hang open as she got the picture. People – Krista couldn't be the only one based on what was happening to her decorations and based on the fact that Hartford was a gossip factory – people thought she was knowingly dating a married man. "He's not married."

Krista appeared doubtful. "But what about that wedding ring he was hiding?"

Was that how the misunderstanding came about? "He was married. He has an ex-wife. I don't know why he had the ring that day. Maybe he was stopping at a pawn shop after work."

"Oh." Krista looked a bit crestfallen.

"And just to be clear. There's nothing going on between me and Jared anyway. When you see him come up here and chat with me... that's the entire extent of our relationship."

"Well, that's boring."

"Yes. It is so boring that we don't need to talk about it ever again." Gaby turned away and didn't even try to look busy. She was soon saved from the awkwardness by customers. Krista was back to talking about herself by the next opportunity.

Gaby felt she should explain things to Jared so she stopped by his office as she passed at the end of the day. She was careful to stay in the doorway and asked if he'd walk out with her.

"Yeah, give me a second." He was moving some papers around on his desk and then clicked a few things on his computer. He stood and grabbed the jacket for his suit from the back of his chair. "Something on your mind?" he asked as they started down the hall together.

"I sort of have a confession."

"Okay?"

"I, um, I told Krista that you're divorced."

"You did?" He sounded disappointed but not angry.

"We were having this really confusing conversation where she accused me and you of sneaking around behind your wife's back and I couldn't let her think that and I know I could have just told her there was nothing going on but... her accusation took me by surprise and... I'm really sorry."

"No, it's okay." He opened the door for her and another coworker. They said goodnight to the extra person and continued towards the parking lot. "I'm not really trying to keep it a secret," Jared said. "I just wasn't... To be honest, gossip about my divorce was a big reason I wanted to leave my last job but I'd rather Krista know the truth than... I'm sorry you got caught up in it."

"Not your fault. Are we still perfectly good acquaintances?" Gaby looked at him hopefully.

"Yes," he said with a smile, "I'm still very happy to be your acquaintance."

"Goodnight." Gaby waved as they split to their respective cars. She was going to run a few errands on her way home. First she needed to stop at the Market for some bread. She didn't *need* bread; she needed to go to the Market. The best way to fight gossip in Hartford was with more gossip. Most people did not spread rumors to be malicious. They just liked information. Gaby wanted to give them *better* information.

She picked up a loaf of bread and a jar of peanut butter as well and took both to the front of the store. "Hey, Mabel," she said.

"Evening, hon. You survive another Monday?"

"It's not quite over yet, is it?"

"I guess not." Mabel smiled vaguely. She looked as though she was working to put something into words and Gaby waited patiently for her to start fishing. "For a long time now I've been expecting you and the older Larrick boy to make an announcement, but maybe I…"

Gaby shook her head. "Owen and I are only friends."

"Mmm… so does that mean there isn't someone special in your life?"

That was the right question. Gaby would normally have given a simple no. This time she leaned in a bit and glanced back to see that no one else was in line. Then she said, "I kind of had my eye on someone but he's still in love with his *ex*-wife."

Mabel's eyes got wider as she nodded. Gaby took her small bag to her car. She hoped this new fact would reach her vandal before any more damage was done. Next she drove – though it was only a block away – to "Things to Do." She didn't plan to get out of the car if the store was still closed. To her surprise, the open sign was facing out.

Gaby parked and approached the front door. The sign with the hours of operation had been taken down and a handwritten sign with bold letters said, "We're open when the sign says open."

That was interesting. Gaby found that the door was unlocked and she opened it to a surprising silence. She took a few steps in and caught sight of Jill in a rocking chair behind her cash register. "Oh, hi," she said as she stood. "I unhooked my contraption for the baby and I can't get used to having to watch for people to enter." Jill was wrapped in pink gingham fabric and she patted the bulge near its center as she stood.

"Oh!" Gaby exclaimed. "Do you have her with you? Can I see?" She took a few cautious steps forward.

"Of course." Jill met her in the middle and pulled back a bit of fabric to show a tiny sleeping face.

"Aww. She is so cute!"

"Thanks."

"How old is she now?"

"Ten days."

"Ten days? And you're already back at work?"

"Sort of. Yesterday was the first day I opened at all and I'm only opening for an hour or two here and there." Jill kept one hand on the baby bump while she talked. "We're still trying to figure out a good schedule but in the meantime, all she does is eat and sleep and she can do both of those right here."

"I bet you're extra grateful for the world's easiest commute."

Jill grinned. "Oh, yeah. No car seat involved." Jill had an easy commute even by Hartford standards. She and Jack lived in the apartment above her store. "Okay," she clapped her hands together suddenly, "to business. You are here for…"

"Yarn," Gaby said to fill in the blank.

"Still knitting?"

"I am actually, but I need yarn for something else right now."

"Very good, very good." Jill began to lead the way to the yarn even though Gaby knew where it was.

There were far fewer shades than would be available at one of the big craft stores in the city. Gaby looked over the three shades of red feeling that none were quite the same as what she had used the first time. Jill seemed to read her thoughts because she said, "I don't think you want red at all."

Gaby picked up one of the reds anyway. She wanted to get started on the wreath that night and she didn't want to drive to Port Harris to do it.

Jill gently took the skein out of Gaby's hand. "Just *look* at the other colors because I can see you're not passionate about this red. That way if you pick something different, your finished project will be different than you pictured instead of not as good as you pictured."

Gaby glanced at the other options to humor Jill. She thought about a green wreath. Everyone had green. Then her eyes fell on a beautiful royal blue. "Oh," she said, "I have some silver ribbon that would go perfect with this."

Jill nodded. "Now we're talking."

Gaby took two skeins of the pretty blue. She'd likely only need one for the wreath but she thought it'd be a good color for a scarf and she still needed a present for her dad. And she didn't know when she might catch Jill open again. She stole another peek at the tiny baby and then went home.

There was a message from Owen when she got home. He'd sent: What happened to your wreath?

She replied: It's gone.

Owen: Did someone take it?

Gaby: Not exactly.

Owen: I ordered pizza. Want to tell me about it while we eat?

Gaby: I still need to change. I'll be over soon.

She was about to put down the phone when it buzzed again. It was her sister, Jess, and there was a slight stab of guilt over her disappointment. Especially since she was on her way to see Owen anyway. Jess sent: Just realized we're coming home on your birthday!! Will there be cake?

Gaby: Tell Mom to make me one. It'd be cheeky if I did it.

Jess replied with a row of smiley faces.

Gaby had walked into her bedroom with the phone. She set it on her dresser and pulled open a drawer. She changed from her stuffy work clothes into comfy and warm black fleece. Then she gathered her supplies for making a new wreath and something for Owen before she knocked on his door.

"Hi," he said as he let her in. His smile faltered as he eyed the bags in her hands.

"Relax," she said. "It's not all for you."

"But some of it is?"

Gaby dropped her yarn and walked over to Owen's kitchen table with the other bag. "I don't know why you look worried."

Owen followed. "Um, maybe because I know you. Please tell me you're not about to throw a handful of glitter all over my kitchen."

"I wouldn't even do that to my own kitchen," Gaby said. She laughed and tried to make it sound indignant. "I love glitter but only when it's attached to something."

"The problem with glitter is that it never stays attached."

Gaby rolled her eyes. "Tiny bits of it are okay. But you still don't need to be worried. There's no glitter on this." She opened the shiny red gift bag that happened to be just the right size to store the decoration she brought. It was a wooden nativity scene. The small stable had a slanted roof and no walls. The figures to place in and around it were each about three inches high. Gaby began to unwrap the pieces.

Owen watched her and said, "That looks familiar."

"It should. And I remember last year you said you liked it."

"I liked it on your table."

Gaby looked up from arranging the sheep long enough to send a playful glare. She knew he was being difficult on purpose.

"It's very nice," Owen conceded, "but I already *have* a nativity scene." He gestured to an end table in his living room.

Gaby snorted at the only decoration she hadn't given Owen. She was pretty sure his mom had put it there. "That tiny thing belongs on a Christmas tree." She checked that the scene was set up appropriately and stuffed the tissue paper back in the bag. Then she faced Owen with both hands on her hips. "Now let's discuss all the reasons you will not be bringing this decoration back to my place."

There were twinges next to Owen's mouth as though he was struggling to keep a straight face while he listened.

"First of all," Gaby said, "I know you like it. And it has no glitter. Also, this is not just something pretty… it has baby Jesus. You cannot return a baby Jesus."

"I might be willing to keep this over here for a couple weeks *if* you're going to be the one to pack it up after Christmas."

"I'm glad you're willing to see reason. Otherwise, I might have had to call your mom."

"My mom? You don't—" A knock interrupted Owen's reaction. "Pizza," he said. He looked happy about the interruption.

Gaby took out two plates while Owen answered the door and they sat on opposite sides of the newly placed nativity scene. Gaby crossed herself and waited for Owen. He said, "Bless us, O Lord, and these Thy gifts, which we are about to receive from Thy bounty, through Christ our Lord. Amen."

"You don't usually go with the traditional prayer," Gaby observed as she helped herself to a slice.

"You don't usually threaten to call my mom."

"You think I'll tattle on you for making up prayers?"

"No. I suppose thinking of her just made me revert. So are you going to tell me what happened to your wreath?" he asked.

"Oh, I guess."

"You guess?"

"Just don't freak out."

90

Owen put down his pizza. "What happened?"

"You're not going to freak out, right?"

"Do you know how much easier it is to freak out when someone says not to."

Gaby sighed. "Someone just… cut it up a bit."

"Someone came to your place with a knife!?"

"Scissors more likely. It's not a big deal. I already bought yarn to make a new one. You can help." She smiled ingratiatingly.

"You're just letting it go? You really need to call the police this time."

Gaby shook her head. "Look… if anything else happens, I'll think about it. But I think I know what's going on so I'm trying something else first."

"When you say you think you know what's going on, does that mean you know who—"

"I have no idea who, but I think it was because of a rumor so I'm trying to fix that."

Owen took a bite of his pizza, not quite as casually as he intended.

"Oh, no." Gaby's face fell. "You've heard it, too?"

"Jimmy heard something. How are you trying to fix it?"

"I stopped at the Market and let something slip to Mabel Thorpe."

"What did you say?"

"I didn't mention any names. I just made sure I used the word ex-wife."

"So he *was* married?"

"I don't know any details about that. I think someone must not have realized it was past tense. Mabel's pretty reliable. I think she'll get that correction out and then no one will care if there's anything going on between us or not."

"But there isn't, right?"

"I already told you that." Gaby looked thoughtful as she worked on her pizza and Owen waited to see if she had anything else to say on the subject. She was quiet for several minutes though.

"Something on your mind?" Owen asked eventually, hoping Jared was not the answer.

"Something else Mabel said. She, um… and it wasn't the first time. She said she thought there was something… something between me and you." Gaby took a deep breath. "And I was wondering if you ever… um…" She stopped and looked nervous.

Owen realized that she was about to ask him if he ever thought about them not just being friends. He wouldn't lie to her but she'd be the one freaking out if he told her the truth. He stuffed half his crust into his mouth to give himself time to choose his words carefully, as Gaby seemed to be doing.

She kept her eyes on her plate and poured the words out quickly when they came to her. "I just wondered if you ever considered the possibility of us, you know, as a couple because sometimes it seems like everyone else in town has that idea."

Owen took a moment even after he swallowed. "Well, I'd be lying if I said it *never* crossed my mind."

"You mean, like, when some nosy person asks you why we're not dating?"

"No, that never happens."

Gaby caught the sarcasm and looked up with a smile. "Of course not," she said. "No one ever asks me either."

"What do you say?" Owen asked. "I mean, when people ask you that."

"Depends who's asking."

"What if it's your mom?"

Gaby's eyes widened before she lowered them again. "Oh, you want a real answer?"

Owen half nodded and half shrugged. If they were going to have this awkward conversation, he hoped he'd at least get some information out of it. He didn't want to make Gaby uncomfortable but if she had a good reason for not wanting to date him, he should probably know about it.

She hesitated. "I don't know," she said at last. "I tell people that I don't know why some people fall in love and some people don't. So anyway, after dinner you get to help me make a new wreath."

"I do?" Owen was catching up to the abrupt subject change.

"Yes. That's the other stuff I brought. I'm going to make a blue one this time. All you need to do is cut the pieces."

"I don't think I need to cut the pieces."

"I think you do."

Owen smiled mischievously. "Will something bad happen to me if I don't help?"

"Yes." Gaby bit her lower lip as she thought fast. "If you only watch, then you'll feel bad about making me do all the work."

"I don't think I'll feel bad about that."

"Then you'll feel left out because it looks like so much fun."

Owen shook his head, still smiling. "Try again."

"If you don't help me… there will be a consequence I won't warn you about ahead of time."

"I see. You're saying I'll need to watch my back."

Gaby smiled slightly and wiggled her eyebrows at him. Owen thought the expression was very attractive. The playful threats were much more fun than simply agreeing to help her, even though they both knew he was going to help. In fact, it was barely a half hour later that he was sitting on his couch cutting segments of blue yarn and laying them between him and Gaby for her to tie to her wreath-in-progress. It was mindless work that he could do while watching TV. And anything that involved sitting next to Gaby was really not a bad way to spend an evening.

Chapter 11

Gaby missed Owen's help on the wreath as she worked on it alone the next night. She wanted to invite him over but couldn't bring herself to do it. Thoughts of him made her alternate between wanting to see him and wanting to hide from him and she had finally admitted what was going on. She wasn't afraid their relationship might change. She was afraid it might not.

He asked her what she told people when they wanted to know why they weren't dating. The last time Gaby's mom asked that question, she had rather flippantly responded that it was because he never asked her out. That was the truth. And now she wondered why he didn't. Was he simply not attracted to her? Did she annoy him too much with all the Christmas stuff? Was there any chance he didn't ask only because he thought she'd say no?

The biggest problem was that Owen was the person Gaby would normally talk to about something that was stressing her out and she couldn't do that. She couldn't say, "Hey, Owen, I think I'm in love with you and I'm freaking out because I don't know how you'd respond if you found out." That was a conversation she did not have the guts to start.

She tried to put it out of her mind while she was at work. Krista's constant blather actually helped. And then as she was leaving for the day, Gaby was reminded of her other problem. She said goodbye to a pair of coworkers who fumbled over their responses. It was obvious that she had interrupted the two of them talking about her. She hadn't heard what they said so it may have been speculation about her involvement with Jared, which wouldn't be terrible if it wasn't classified as involvement as "the other woman." She still hoped to quickly reached the day people were not talking about her at all.

Gaby stopped her car in front of her apartment and sighed heavily before she turned it off. It was good to be home, even if it made her go right back to thinking about Owen.

"Hey, Gaby," a voice called as soon as she climbed out of her driver's seat.

She looked up and saw Seth Anderson jogging across the street towards her. "Hi, Seth," she said with a nod. They'd been neighbors long enough for her to know what was coming next.

"What can I help you with?" he asked.

She let out a short laugh. Seth wasn't really trying to be helpful. He was trying to escape from some very talkative retirees across the street. It was sweet that he visited them regularly but she didn't appreciate the pressure of being his getaway excuse. Once they popped the hood on her car, though nothing was wrong and Seth knew no more about cars than she did. Another time he brought her to his door and handed over a dying houseplant. He told her to pretend she was going to nurse it back to health for him but was welcome to toss it if she couldn't work any magic.

"I don't know, Seth," Gaby said. "I don't—"

"What about that box?" He pointed into her backseat. "Can I carry that for you?"

"No. That's just some old papers I was going to recycle at work. I keep forgetting to bring them in with me."

"I'll take them." He tried to open the car door. It was locked.

"What are you going to do with my scraps?"

He shrugged. "I can recycle it just as easily at my office. Let's move the box to my car."

Gaby unlocked her back door and Seth reached in and picked up the box. She locked up and followed him to his car. "You know this is a ridiculous charade, right? You could just tell Walt and Carol that you need to leave."

"What would be the fun in that?" Seth asked. "Besides, this way they think I'm a very helpful young man." He said the last few words as though he was quoting the neighbors. "I have to think of my reputation."

Seth winked at Gaby as he shifted the box to open the trunk of his car. She was aware of his reputation. The charming flirt had broken more hearts than anyone in Hartford cared to count.

"Well," Gaby said, "I sure appreciate you inventing a way to help me."

"Hey, do you appreciate it enough to have dinner with me tonight?" Seth appeared to hold his breath as he waited hopefully for her answer.

Gaby began to shake her head before an idea came to her. Perhaps being out with Seth would be another way to help squash that rumor. "What do you have in mind?" she asked him.

Seth closed his trunk and turned to her, grinning as though she'd agreed. "You picked a good time to say yes. We have a top secret mission to accomplish tonight." He sent a few shifty glances over her shoulder. "But first we need to discuss what you're wearing."

Gaby instinctively looked down at her dress. She had decided it was Christmasy because it matched the bright blue of her wreath. Her gray coat was unbuttoned. Seth was wearing a black suit but his striped tie was hanging loose and the top button on his shirt was undone. She had a feeling he was going to say they both needed to be more casual.

Seth made a show of looking her up and down. "You look *fantastic* but that dress attracts too much attention and you can't run in heels."

"Um… why would I need to run?"

"Make sure you pick out something comfortable with dark colors."

"Dark colors?" Gaby said. "Why are you making it sound like we're going to do something illegal?"

"Not illegal. Just secret." Seth wiggled his eyebrows and then shooed Gaby towards the stairs to her apartment. "Now go change and I'll pick you up in ten minutes because I'm hungry."

"All right." Gaby didn't know what she was getting herself into, but Seth wouldn't really do anything against the law and he might provide an evening of distraction. If she stayed home, she'd spend the whole time warring with herself over contacting Owen or how to respond if he texted her.

She went into her apartment and put on some flannel-lined jeans and a dark green Hartford fleece that would keep her warm and comfortable. And still looked cute. This might not be a date but that was no reason to slack on her appearance. She twisted a few curls around her fingers to smooth them and stuffed only the essentials into her pocket so she could leave her purse behind. She didn't want to mess with it if she found herself running, though she hoped Seth had only been teasing about that part.

96

He knocked on her door just as she was ready for him.

"You still look fantastic," he said. "But now you look ready for fun. Shall we go?" Seth made an elaborate sweep with his arm to allow Gaby to head down the stairs first. He motioned to his car as they reached the bottom. "I'll drive. You okay with pizza?"

"Sure. What else do you have planned?"

He opened his passenger door for her and put on a puzzled expression. "What makes you think I have something else planned?"

"Oh, I don't know," Gaby said, "something about a top secret mission and shoes I can run in."

Seth grinned and looked at her shoes. "Nice choice, by the way."

"Thanks," she mumbled as he closed the door for her. When he got behind the wheel and started up the car, Gaby tried again to get some specifics on the evening. "Are you going to tell me about this mission?"

He gave her a playful glance. "Do you not understand the word secret?"

"I can't help if you don't tell me."

"I'll tell you," he said. "But not yet."

Gaby sighed at Seth. He continued to display his adorable dimples. She felt overmatched.

The drive to Pops was only a few minutes. Seth parked and ran around to open the door for her again. It might be best to clarify the evening once they were seated. She knew it was his standard operating procedure but he was acting too much like a date for her not to say something. Seth led her to the last red booth on the right side of the restaurant and allowed her to choose a side.

A young man with spiked blonde hair immediately plopped a pair of menus on the table.

"Hey, Anthony," Seth said. "What are you doing out of the kitchen?"

The man gave a bored shrug. "We're short today so I'm stuck taking orders. You guys want a Hartford Special?"

Gaby shook her head at Seth. He looked back at Anthony. "We'll need a minute."

Anthony walked off without another word.

Seth tilted his head at Gaby. "I don't think you can wear a

Hartford shirt and *not* get a Hartford Special."

"I think I can."

"You know, I bet they'd give us a date version with no onions if that's what you're worried about."

"You know this is not a real date, right?"

"Of course it's not a date *yet*." Gaby's hand was on the table and Seth reached across and began to draw small circles on the back of it with his fingertip. "I haven't done any wooing yet."

Gaby gave a disapproving look to his hand. "There won't be any wooing."

Seth continued to touch her hand for a few moments before he sat back. "Okay," he said, "I know you didn't just suddenly realize I'm a fun guy. What made you say yes tonight?"

"I guess you could say I'm on something of a mission myself."

"Really?" Seth tipped one eyebrow up with interest.

"There's, um... there's been some talk about me lately. I suppose you've heard the one about me seeing a married guy?"

Seth shook his head. "I don't pay any attention to rumors. Otherwise, I might think I had the attention span of a gnat."

Gaby might have been uncomfortable – she'd helped spread that rumor – if Seth hadn't looked completely unconcerned by it. She envied his confidence even as it made her laugh. "Well, I'm trying to kill the rumor about me because it's not true and I hoped maybe if I was seen with... someone else." She looked at him apologetically because she was admitting that she wanted to use him.

Seth gasped and immediately jumped from his seat. For a second, she thought she'd offended him. Then he came over and squeezed in next to her. "I'm glad you told me," he said. "Now I can be your accomplice. It's more convincing if we sit next to each other and you should try to look adoringly at me from time to time."

"Seth, you're too much."

"That's why we're so good together. Right, honey?"

Anthony stepped up to their table and said, "You decided?" He might have been stifling a yawn.

"Oh, not yet." Gaby hastily opened her menu.

"We got distracted," Seth said with a suggestive look at Gaby. She felt herself blushing. He played the part a little too well.

Anthony suddenly focused on Gaby and looked less bored. "What's going on here?" he asked. "I thought you were dating Owen Larrick."

She tried to shake her head casually. Seth leaned over and whispered. "Another reason I don't pay attention to rumors."

She conceded his point with a smile.

"Don't waste your time with this guy," Anthony said with a nod to Seth. "You should let me take you out sometime."

Anthony didn't have the charisma to make his comment sound like a joke. He sounded as though he was asking Gaby out right in front of her date while indicating that he would not have done so if it was Owen. Gaby was afraid Anthony was about to receive a fist somewhere unpleasant and she felt bad for thinking that he would deserve it. But then Seth smiled at her and asked what she liked on her pizza.

"Pepperoni?"

"Regular pizza or square?"

"Regular."

"Great," Seth said. "Nice and simple." He put his arm along the booth behind Gaby before he looked at Anthony. "Large pepperoni."

"You sure?" Anthony asked. He was still looking at Gaby as though she might address his other comment.

"Large pepperoni," she repeated.

Anthony walked away looking slightly puzzled, as though he either didn't realize he had been ignored or didn't understand why.

"Sorry about that," Gaby said.

"Don't worry, you just need to practice those adoring looks." Seth appeared to demonstrate on her before he added, "You're also welcome to put your hand on my knee when he comes back."

"Seth." Gaby said his name like a mother warning a child that he was about to get himself grounded.

He laughed at her tone and said, "It's a standing offer." Then he asked about her plans for Christmas. Gaby being Gaby, they didn't need another topic for the rest of the meal.

Seth insisted on paying. He said he didn't want anyone calling him cheap whether it was a real date or not. Gaby let him put his arm around her waist as they walked out, mostly because Anthony was watching. She began walking towards his car before Seth steered her the other way.

"Why are we walking back?" Gaby asked.

"Have you forgotten the secret mission?"

"I was beginning to think that was all talk."

"What?!" Seth withdrew his arm to put both hands up in the air in an exaggerated show of shock. "You wound me with your accusations of dishonesty. We just needed to fuel up first."

"All right. Where are we going?"

"This way." Seth started walking.

"Are you going to be more specific?"

He grinned. "You'll see when we get there."

Gaby remembered the last time someone had suggested she'd need dark-colored clothing. "Just promise me that this mission does not involve toilet paper."

"Oh, please," Seth groaned. "How juvenile do you think I am? We're going to steal a wise man."

"What?!" Gaby stopped walking and Seth turned around in front of her.

"Okay, not steal," he said. "We're going to... *relocate* a wise man.

She stood still and raised both eyebrows at him.

"Come on." Seth beckoned encouragingly and began to explain as Gaby started walking again, slowly. "There's a prank war at my office. I can tell that Mr. Bennett wants to get someone but is worried people will be afraid to retaliate against the boss. I'm going to do him the favor of getting him first."

"By stealing a wise man?"

"I misspoke. We're just going to remove it from his yard so I can take it to work with me in the morning."

That did sound fairly harmless. Especially considering that Mr. Bennett was not Gaby's boss. She found herself smiling at the impending caper as the house came into view. The Bennetts lived in a large brick house only a block from Pops. Gaby always appreciated their very fine Christmas display. The front of the house was outlined with strings of white lights wrapped with greenery. Red bows were tied to the top of each banister along the porch and big wreaths with more lights hung from every window. And in the very center of the front yard was a detailed and well-lit nativity scene. Well-lit. She stopped again and looked at Seth.

100

"There's a giant spotlight on that nativity scene," she said.

"That's why we're wearing running shoes." Seth took her hand. "Just relax. First we're going to casually walk past as though we are two lovebirds on a stroll. Then we'll double back and swipe it."

Gaby nodded and looked at the display again. "Which wise man are we going for?"

Seth studied the scene. "I think... the one closest to the front, with the sort of square container. Do you suppose that's frankincense or myrrh?"

"Definitely myrrh. Do you think it's very heavy?"

"Looks like plastic to me," Seth said.

Gaby nodded. She'd go along, but Seth was going to have to grab it himself no matter how light it was. They walked past a few more houses before they turned around. Seth was still holding her hand and swinging their arms between them. As they reached the edge of the Bennetts' property, Seth said, "I'm going to start a countdown. When I get to one we run up, grab the wise man, run to the far corner of the lawn, and then restart the casual walk. Ready?"

"I guess." Gaby took a deep breath.

"Three... two... one!"

Seth ran and pulled Gaby along. He let go as they arrived at the crèche. He tried to pick up the wise man and found that it was hollow and had a sandbag stuffed into the bottom to keep it upright. He muttered something unintelligible and in her panic, Gaby accidentally knocked Joseph over. She righted the honorable carpenter as Seth pulled the sandbag free. They jumped up together and knocked into each other, which caused Seth to take out a defenseless shepherd.

"I think you'd have been better off without my help," Gaby observed as she fixed the display again.

Seth grinned and shook his head. "Everything is better with a beautiful woman by your side."

Gaby was too busy racing back to the sidewalk to comment on the remark. The whole escapade had taken no more than ten seconds but the possibility of getting caught made that enough time to get her heart fully pumping. She reached the sidewalk first and tried to slow herself to a walk. Seth resumed the casual stroll they'd been on even though he was now carrying a two-foot tall plastic figure. He looked fairly satisfied with himself and Gaby was trying to contain her giggles.

Then he said, "Uh-oh," and passed the wise man to Gaby before she realized that he was looking at a police car parked just ahead of them.

Gaby felt more embarrassment than fear as the passenger door of the car opened and Jimmy Larrick stepped out to wait for them.

"Why did you give it to me?" she whispered.

"Trust me," Seth said.

Jimmy gave Gaby a serious look as she stopped in front of him. He glanced pointedly at the wise man in her arms and then raised an eyebrow at her. "May I ask what you two are up to tonight?"

"Um, we're just taking a walk." She knew it sounded like forced innocence.

"You know how much Gaby loves her Christmas decorations," Seth said. "She can't ever leave home without *something* Christmasy." He, on the other hand, sounded thoroughly genuine as a guy explaining that Gaby just liked to carry plastic statues around town.

Jimmy shook his head. "I'm going to make a mental note of this picture in case anyone asks later."

"Why would anyone ask?" Seth said. "Everyone knows Gaby's a Christmas nut." He winked at her.

"Actually, Gaby, that's sort of why we stopped," Jimmy said with a tilt of his head towards the car he'd left, and presumably the other officer who comprised the we in his statement. "We unofficially caught the person who broke your lights and we can keep it unofficial if you want. But I thought you'd like to know that he or she is underage and very very sorry."

"Thanks, Jimmy," she said. "You didn't have to bother."

"I did," he said calmly and she knew he meant that Owen had insisted.

Seth laughed. "Jimmy, did you scare the kid straight? I'd have liked to have seen that."

"Joe talked to h— the kid."

"Too bad. I love the thought of you striking fear into some poor kid."

Jimmy rolled his eyes. "Why is that amusing?"

"It just is. Hey, can you guys do me a favor?" Seth asked.

Jimmy looked at the wise man in Gaby's arms. "I think I'm already doing you a favor."

"I know you don't usually pay much attention to the meters downtown," Seth totally ignored the insinuation, "but Anthony Meyers is parked out front and I think he's going to be too busy to feed the meter. Don't you think he should save those spaces for customers?"

"I assume he did something to make you concerned about his parking?"

Seth gave a serious nod. The earlier slight must have bothered him more than he let on at the time.

"No promises, man, but I'll see what we can do," Jimmy said. He waved at both of them and climbed back into the police car.

Gaby shoved the wise man back into Seth's hands. "You could have told him you were carrying it for me."

"He didn't make us put it back, did he?" He showed her the dimples without even smiling. It was as though he knew they were irresistible and just slipped them out of his pocket when he needed to charm her.

Gaby quietly started walking back to Pops. Seth placed the wise man in his trunk with the box of Gaby's old school papers. It made a curious tableau of their evening. He took her home and they walked up to the shared building together.

"Have you checked out my Christmas decorations?" Seth asked.

Of the four apartments, Seth's was the only one that didn't have a single string of lights. Gaby couldn't see anything on his door either. "You don't have any decorations," she said.

"Come see." He inclined his head towards his front door.

"I'm not coming in," she said.

"You won't have to." Seth grinned. "Unless you change your mind."

Gaby couldn't help her interest in potential trimmings so she followed him to his porch. When he looked up, she immediately laughed at her own gullibility. "I can't believe I didn't see that coming. I should have known you'd have mistletoe."

"Ready when you are," he said.

Any Christmas tradition was sacred in Gaby's book. She stood on her toes to meet Seth for a very quick, very chaste kiss. He responded by closing his eyes and putting his hand on his chest.

"Be still my heart."

She sighed at his antics. "Someday, you're going to have to be serious."

"I tried serious once," he said. "Didn't take."

"Goodnight, Seth."

"Goodnight, Gaby."

"And thanks for the pizza," she said as she turned to head up the stairs.

"You're welcome. And you know where to find me when you want to do it again."

Chapter 12

It was not a date. Those were the words Owen read on his phone and they did not make the uncomfortable feeling in his chest any less uncomfortable. He had thought Gaby seemed calmer when they were last together. And she had asked him if he ever thought about the two of them dating, which meant *she* had thought about it. The fact that she didn't laugh off the idea or explain why it wouldn't work gave him hope.

That was Monday though. She already had plans to come to his place on Friday and Saturday so he assumed he'd end up at her apartment sometime midweek. But as he got through Tuesday, Wednesday, and now most of Thursday without hearing a single word from her that hope had begun to fizzle. It was beginning to feel again like she was trying to create distance. He was convincing himself to stop worrying and just call her when he got a text from his brother.

Jimmy sent: `You can relax.  Identified and warned Gaby's vandal.  Told Gaby already.`

Owen: `Just now?`

Jimmy: `Last night.  Bumped into her near Pops.`

Owen: `Was she alone?`

Of course that was a nosy question but Owen didn't have anything to hide from his brother so he thought he might as well be blunt. That was when Jimmy had replied: `It was not a date.`

That only partly answered his question. It meant she was not alone but it didn't tell him who she was with. It meant the other person was a guy but didn't tell him how Jimmy knew it wasn't a date. Then Jimmy texted two more words: `Ask Gaby.`

Two little words were enough to make Owen feel like a coward for hesitating to call Gaby. He texted her first with: `Are you home?`

Instead of a reply on his phone, he heard a familiar knock on the wall. That was the knock that meant Gaby was on the other side of it. Owen knew her apartment so well that it was easy to imagine he could see right through the wall to Gaby sitting on her couch.

Owen's phone rang before he could make the call. "Hey, Gaby, what are you up to tonight?"

"Oh, you know I'm watching one of those Christmas love stories."

That would have been his guess. "I'm so sorry I interrupted a work of cinematic art."

"Don't be," Gaby said with a disgruntled note in her voice. "This one is starting to frustrate me."

"How so?"

"They have the girl dating this guy that everyone else knows is a jerk while the nice guy is hanging around waiting for her to figure things out. They're going to make us wait the whole two hours when it's so obvious who she's supposed to be with."

"And that's frustrating to *watch*?" Owen winced at the tone that threatened to be a little obvious itself. Gaby didn't seem to notice.

"Yeah. I mean you don't need to make the girl look like an idiot for dating the jerk. There are better ways to delay the happy ending."

Owen had enough of that topic. "Did you finish your new wreath yet?" he asked.

"Just tonight. I'll hang it in the morning for you to admire."

"Great. Jimmy mentioned that he saw you *near* Pops last night. I thought that was an odd word choice. Were you actually at Pops?"

"Yeah. We ate first."

"Um… we?"

There was a pause before Gaby said, "I went with Seth."

"Seth? Seth Anderson?" Owen had been prepared for her to say Jared. He was trying to accept that she could be friends with two guys at once. But Seth Anderson did not do *just friends*. "You went out with that slimy—"

"Easy, Owen. I know you're not a fan but he's not that bad. And I didn't *go out* with him. We mostly just had dinner."

Mostly? She'd been with Seth and they mostly had dinner? Gaby had said more than once that Seth was fun for occasional flirting but that she'd never again go out with him. This was not a change that Owen expected or wanted. "All he does is spout insincere flattery. What made you decide to have dinner with him?"

"Well... it was just once and I told him that. It wasn't a date. I just thought... It sounds kind of dumb now because I realize that anyone who believes I'd date a married guy would believe I'd date two guys at once but I thought if people saw me with someone else then that would disassociate me with Jared."

So she just wanted people to see her with a guy and couldn't think of one. Did Gaby not understand how that was worse than if she actually liked Seth? Owen closed his mouth on that question and tried to swallow it while he asked, "What does mostly mean?"

"Huh?"

"I mean what else did you do with Seth?"

"Oh," Gaby chuckled to herself. "We stole a wise man."

"What does that mean?"

"We took a wise man from Mr. Bennett's nativity scene as a prank."

"You attacked someone else's decorations after what happened to you?"

"Owen!" Gaby sounded a bit hurt. "It wasn't the same thing at all. We didn't do any damage and Seth called me this morning to say how hard Mr. Bennett laughed when he found the thing on his desk."

It wasn't the same. Owen knew he was trying to pick a fight because he was annoyed. That wasn't going to help anything. "You're right," he said. "I'm sorry. I'm glad you had fun with Seth."

"Thanks. But it was definitely one time. You know what he did at the end?"

"What?"

Gaby sighed. "I should have known better but he tricked me into getting under some mistletoe."

Hearing that someone else got her under the mistletoe first was the last straw. Owen said, rather roughly, "You do know that I'm a guy, right?"

"What?! Where did that come from?"

Gaby was laughing and that didn't help, but Owen tried to rein in the frustration. Yelling at Gaby wasn't going to change anything. It certainly wouldn't keep her happy if he vented all the ways she made their relationship difficult without knowing it. He waded back into the conversation more carefully. "It's just that you said you wanted people to see you with a guy and people see you with me all the time."

Gaby's laugh cut off sharply. "Oh," she said. "I get it."

Did she? Owen tried to be patient while he waited to see if she actually understood that she'd made him jealous. Maybe he shouldn't have said anything.

"I already said it was kind of a dumb idea," Gaby said. "And I just happened to think of it when Seth was standing in front of me. If I had been alone when I thought I needed a guy for something, you would definitely have been the first one I thought of. And then you could have had the pleasure of pretending to be my date."

She was placating him because she thought she'd insulted his masculinity. Sure, that was part of it and it was nice to know she hadn't sought Seth out for the job. But Owen didn't want to pretend to be Gaby's date and he didn't want to think about what Seth might have done to fill that part. "Jimmy also said he caught your vandal," Owen said.

"Sounds like it was just a kid. Can I gloat now about being right that it was nothing to worry about?"

"No. People can still get hurt even when that isn't the intention."

"You're right. I wasn't going to gloat anyway." Gaby drew a slow breath. "You know, I am glad I have you to worry about me and protect me from stuff, even when you imagine the threat."

"And you're glad I bought a Christmas tree birthday cake today?"

"Yea!" Gaby let out a little squeal. It was a happy sound. "Should I come over right after work tomorrow?"

"Whenever you're ready," he said.

****

Gaby walked into the bank Friday morning knowing that it was her last day of work before Christmas and that gave it a different feel than usual, almost like the last day of school before summer vacation. Krista was the same though.

"Gabrielle, have you seen Mr. Chapman today?"

"Yeah, why?"

"Did you see his tie?"

"Reindeer hanging stockings, right?"

Krista clicked her tongue. "Can you believe that?"

"No," Gaby said with a smile, "I don't believe that reindeer can hang stockings."

Krista rolled her eyes. "I mean, can you believe he's wearing that?"

"Christmas is less than a week away. Why is a Christmas tie weird?"

"Because he'd old!"

"Too old to celebrate Christmas?"

"No," Krista said. "Just too old for silly stuff."

"I hope I'm never too old for silly stuff."

"I'm pretty sure you'll be doing silly Christmas stuff for many, many years." That was a masculine voice. Jared had arrived.

"I still haven't gotten used to you jumping into the middle of a conversation," Gaby said to him before she turned on Krista. "And why don't you ever warn me?"

"It's more fun this way." Krista smiled as Jared positioned himself between the two women. "Jared will have no one to sneak up on next week."

"You don't think Maryann would appreciate that?" Gaby asked. Maryann was the name of the person filling in for Gaby during her vacation. Maryann was all business and Gaby wondered how she and Krista would survive each other. But she didn't plan to think about it at all while she was gone.

"When you were sick last month that woman refused to talk to me at all," Krista said. "She is so boring."

"Well, it'll be a short week for everyone at least," Gaby said.

"By the way, Gaby, you look especially nice today. Are you dressing up for your birthday a day early?" Jared asked.

"You remembered!"

"And as far as you know, I did it without the reminder."

Krista laughed. "Neither of us believes that. Men never remember birthdays."

Jared opened his mouth as though he was about to defend either himself or his whole gender when he was interrupted by the entrance of a customer. "Good day, ladies," he said instead as he

109

slipped away.

A woman with gray curly hair and a red coat approached Gaby with a deposit. She was Mabel's sister-in-law. "Hello, Mrs. Thorpe," Gaby greeted her.

"Afternoon, hon. Are you staying warm?"

"So far. It's backwards day though." It had been much colder when she went home for lunch than when she left in the morning.

The older woman finished her transaction and then leaned in with a conspiratorial whisper. "A man who holds on is a good catch. You just have to wait for the right timing."

Gaby tried to nod at the advice as though it was meant more generally than it was. Even though the story had become more sympathetic, she was still hoping to reach the day people stopped talking about her altogether.

Jared stopped by again near the end of the day to wish her a happy birthday because he didn't get a chance to say the actual words the first time. He and everyone who knew she wouldn't be back wished her a merry Christmas on her way out for the day. Krista told her not to have too much fun.

Gaby checked her phone and found a message from Owen. It said: The new wreath looks great. You can really tell I helped.

She smiled as she put the phone down and examined her reflection in her bedroom mirror. She was not going to change her clothes. That was as far as her plan had come so far. It wasn't even really a plan so much as a hope, a hope that her relationship with Owen would shift naturally if she acted like they were dating.

Seth had given her the idea, though he didn't know that. When he held her hand or put his arm around her, there had been tiny sparks. Not sparks that said she was particularly attracted to Seth, just reminders that being touched by a guy was different than being touched by, say, a family member. Gaby wondered what would happen if Owen were reminded of that. She didn't know how to go about this reminder that she wasn't his sister beyond her appearance but planned to be open to opportunities. She was, at least at the particular moment, feeling some optimism about their chances. They were good together and something about the previous night's phone call made her think Owen wouldn't be too hard to persuade.

She had put on her favorite dress before work. Dressing up right before visiting Owen would be too obvious. The dress was fairly conservative and therefore appropriate for working in a bank but more figure-flattering than some of her others. And several people had said that the dark red was one of her best colors. She ran her fingers through her hair to separate some of her curls and decided that she looked pretty good.

The temperature had continued to drop and dipped below freezing shortly before dusk. It was dark and seriously brisk when Gaby hugged herself for a bit of warmth as she rushed across the shared porch. Her stomach fluttered nervously as she knocked on Owen's door. She wanted him to notice that she looked nicer than usual without saying anything. She was afraid her birthday excuse might sound like an excuse.

Owen was smiling when he opened the door, but then he sighed as he moved aside for her. "Why don't you ever wear a coat?"

Gaby hurried inside. "I do," she said. "Just not when I visit you."

"Is it really that much of a bother to put on a coat?"

"It kind of is. And I don't remember the last time you wore a coat to visit me."

"Yeah, but I don't arrive with my teeth chattering. You could at least wear something with long sleeves. Though you do look very nice, by the way."

"I thought I'd stay in my work clothes since it's a special occasion."

"It is?" Owen feigned surprise. "Are we celebrating something today?"

"I think you know the answer to that."

"Maybe I do. But here's something I don't know the answer to…"

"What?" she prompted.

"Why did you bring Christmas Pig?" He nodded at the small stuffed animal in her hands.

"Because I thought he'd look even cuter on your couch."

"Come on, Gaby, you can't bring me something when it's *your* birthday. And pigs aren't red."

"This one is." Gaby set the pig on a corner of Owen's couch

111

and turned back with a satisfied smile. "He looks very happy here," she said.

"Do you know that the smile is stitched to the pig's face?"

"Don't worry. I can still tell when he's happy."

"*You* look very happy here, as a matter of fact. Good day at work?"

"Last day. For a week. Put that with my birthday and almost Christmas and... Yes. Definitely happy."

"Okay. Come with me while I work on dinner." Owen motioned for her to follow him to the kitchen.

"What are we having?"

"Chicken and rice and broccoli."

"That sounds healthier than usual."

"Don't worry. We'll ruin it with cake."

"Ah, cake." Gaby bounced on her heels slightly. She glanced around the kitchen. Owen already had some chicken in a pan and was pulling a bunch of broccoli out of his refrigerator. That tiny ball of red glitter was still on the back of his counter and her latest addition was... "Owen," she said, "what have you done to the nativity scene?"

"Huh?" He turned to look and then smiled sheepishly. "It's hard not to play with it when it's sitting right in front of me."

"You put baby Jesus on the roof," she said indignantly.

"Well, it's slanted so the standing guys fall off."

Gaby started putting the pieces back in order. "You have Mary out tending sheep and oh my goodness... the camel is standing on an angel. I think you've just broken a commandment."

Owen had his back to her but she could tell he was laughing. "I'm pretty sure there's no commandment against rearranging a nativity scene."

"You better hope not." She hoped that he didn't point out she was guilty of almost the same thing.

Once baby Jesus was safely indoors and being properly witnessed, Gaby returned her attention to her birthday dinner and the guy who was preparing it. Owen was wearing jeans and a plain blue shirt and he looked good without trying. He was surprisingly well built for a computer geek who as far as she knew never visited a gym. She thought she could enjoy that for a few moments while he was busy.

But he said, "It feels like you're staring at me. Am I underdressed for this special occasion or something?"

"Just watching you work. Can I help?"

"Um… you can put the candles in the cake if you want." He nodded towards the end of the short counter. A cake in the shape of a Christmas tree with light green frosting and colorful sprinkles was in a white box. Gaby noted the familiar Hartford Market sticker on top as she removed the lid and opened the first box of candles. She tried to spread them around the cake like real lights even though she knew that putting them closer together would likely make them easier to blow out. Owen continued to chop broccoli at her side.

"How was your day at work?" Gaby asked.

"Fine."

"I think I detected a sigh in that fine. Was it not entirely fine?"

"Well, a certain person was having some issues and you know how she always wants a play-by-play of what I'm doing."

"Of course. I'm familiar with your favorite coworker."

"She's really not that bad except when I have to hang out at her desk. She doesn't seem to understand that most of us don't say every thought that pops into our heads so she thinks I'm not trying to fix the problem if I'm not telling her everything I'm trying to do."

"Maybe you could just make up stuff the whole time."

"You mean like tell her I'm trying to realign the lithium crystals so the hyperdrive motivator can talk to the quantum matrix?" Owen paused to see if she approved of his nonsense. "Or maybe that the motherboard is ray-shielded so I need to generate a psionic field to reactivate the spacial signal."

"Oh my goodness! You are such a nerd."

"You're the one who told me to make something up."

"But you did it way too easily and… oh, nuts."

"What?"

"You made me lose count."

"Why are you counting the candles?"

Gaby gave him a look that said he'd asked a dumb question. "You know how birthday candles work, right? I'm twenty-six so that's how many candles go on the cake."

"But you don't have to count them. Just put on a whole box plus two more."

"How do you know there are twenty-four in a box?"

"It says so right there." He pointed at the box on the counter with the knife he was using.

"That might be wrong."

"Oh, I see. You just *need* to count the candles." Owen rolled his eyes at her. "Now who's a nerd?"

"You are not allowed to call me names on my birthday."

"Technically, your birthday is not until tomorrow."

"Technically, there's cake. That makes it my birthday."

"There will be cake if you ever get the candles on it." He turned away from her to push the broccoli from the cutting board into the pan.

"Stop making me lose count then."

She placed exactly the right amount of candles without further interruptions and Owen lit them when they were done eating. He refused to sing Happy Birthday by himself but played the tune on his phone and then reminded her to make a wish. Gaby managed to get them all out, though she thought she might be turning blue by the last one. "Whew," she said. "I wished for the first piece."

"Oh, no."

"What?"

"Your wish isn't supposed to come true if you tell me, but I'm not sure I can *not* give you the first piece."

"That's okay. I might be lying about what I wished for."

"That would be kind of a lame wish," Owen said as he dished out a slice and handed the plate to Gaby.

"Are you mocking my wish?"

"You said that wasn't your wish."

"Maybe it was and maybe it wasn't." Gaby tried to look mysterious as she forked a bite of cake into her mouth. It was chocolate and it was delicious. She hadn't made a wish at all. But if she had, she'd have wished for many more evenings like the one they were having.

Gaby helped Owen clean up after dinner and then they went to the next room to relax in front of the TV. "Owen?" she said as she looked at the list.

"Yeah, yeah… I recorded whatever sappy movie was on last night *only* because it's your birthday."

"Well, I'd hate for you to think you made a sweet gesture for nothing."

"I think I get points for the gesture whether you take advantage of it or not."

Gaby smiled at him while she considered. "We should watch it," she said.

He didn't say anything while he started the movie. He was glad she seemed excited about it. Every now and then she would claim one of those movies looked terrible. Since they all sounded exactly the same to him, he couldn't be sure this wasn't one of the outliers.

It was somewhere around halfway through when Owen completely gave up even trying to pay attention. He couldn't bring himself to care which guy the heroine was going to end up with when it had taken him at least a half hour to realize there were two different guys. His attention landed on Gaby instead. She really did look wonderful. Her dress was nice, but it was mostly the constant smiling he noticed. It seemed that whatever had been bothering her had passed. Perhaps she'd been more upset by the rumors or the vandalism than she'd let on.

He stretched his arm along the back of the couch to reach a lock of her hair. He tugged it straight and watched it spring back a few times, knowing she'd swat his hand away in a minute. She appeared mildly amused but when he thought the admonishment was coming, she said, "That looks like an invitation."

"What does?"

Gaby smiled yet again as she slipped off her shoes. Then she moved a bit closer while she tucked her legs up next to her and leaned back into the crook of his arm. Her eyes barely left the movie.

Owen felt his head spinning. She was soft and she smelled like… sugar cookies? That was perfectly Gaby, sweet and Christmasy. But what was she doing? She had fallen asleep on his shoulder once – a very fond memory – but there was nothing to interpret about being tired.

She'd never done anything like this before. Was she so comfortable in their friendship that she was oblivious to the thoughts that would run rampant in his mind with her pressed up against his side? Or did she mean to accept an invitation to get closer? The only thing he knew for sure was that she didn't mean to be incredibly frustrating. She probably thought things were perfectly clear one way or the other. He could be happy with comfortable unless he was missing out on... wait. She was talking to him.

"Owen," she said again.

"What?"

"Commercial."

"Oh, sorry." He picked up the remote to fast forward.

"You're not paying any attention, are you?"

"Sure I am. She's going to end up with that guy who helped her carry the Christmas tree, right?"

He felt Gaby sigh before she said, "That's her brother."

"Oh, right. I was just kidding." That's what he got for taking a guess. There were apparently three guys in this movie.

Gaby laughed. "No, you weren't. But it's okay. The fact that you're not enjoying yourself makes it that much nicer that you're willing to watch with me."

The movie restarted and Owen didn't correct her. Just because he didn't like the movie didn't mean he wasn't enjoying himself. He decided that if she could get comfortable then he could, too. He let his arm drop slightly from the back of the couch across her shoulders. That was more comfortable and that's what he'd tell her if she had anything to say about it. She did not. She didn't even seem to notice.

Owen turned off the TV when the movie ended and waited for Gaby to say or do something. She sat up slowly without looking at him. She leaned forward to put her shoes back on and then turned to him while she was still bent over. "I guess I should head back. Unless you've changed your mind and want to give me a present now." She flashed a bright smile.

Owen shook his head. "I couldn't if I wanted to. It isn't here."

"It's not here?" She looked around the room as though there might be something covered in wrapping paper that she missed earlier. "But you'll have it tomorrow?" she asked.

"That's why you can't come over before ten."

Gaby's face lit up and she opened her mouth to say something.

"And I'm not giving you any more hints."

"I guess I can wait one more day." She stood and stretched slightly. Owen jumped up and opened his bedroom door. He returned a few seconds later carrying his jacket. "Put this on and wear it back in the morning." He held it up for her to put her arms in.

"You're bossy all of a sudden." Gaby smiled though and complied with the request before she opened his front door. Then she made a sound between a gasp and a squeal and unnecessarily explained, "It's snowing!"

Owen took a step closer for a better look. The flakes were large and falling slowly. There were a few white patches on the ground but most of it was melting on contact.

Gaby was staring at a house across the street that was decked out in colorful Christmas lights with an inflatable snowman on the lawn. "It's so pretty," she said. "There's something about snow that makes all the decorations that much more... magical." She turned back to see if Owen agreed.

He wasn't looking at the snow. There was something in his eyes that made her forget all about it as well. Was that real or was she projecting her own feelings? That adoring look that Seth trotted out had nothing on Owen's expression. His eyes dropped to her mouth only for a second. That was long enough to communicate his desire. Gaby was aware of only two things. The best friend she'd ever had was about to kiss her and her heart was trying to break right out of her chest in anticipation of it.

Then Owen blinked and pulled back. "You, um... you need to get inside before you freeze," he said. "You can watch from the window."

Gaby felt her head moving up and down in a nod. But she did not agree at all that she needed to move. "Yeah, I... Goodnight, Owen." She ran to her apartment and leaned against the inside of her door while she tried to breathe. Owen's scent was on his jacket and its weight almost felt as though he was still there. She kept it on as she found a good window to watch the snow. It had already begun to taper off. After a minute, she went to check her phone. Her dress had no pockets so she had left it on her dresser.

There was a text from her mom that said only: noon!!!!!

117

That was a not-so-subtle reminder of what time she was expected at her parents' house the next day. She had also missed a call from her sister by only a few minutes. She called Hannah back.

"Gaby," she said as she answered, "how's the weather in Hartford?"

"Did you really call me to ask about the weather?"

"Sadly, yes. I just had a bizarre conversation with Mom where I couldn't tell if she was more upset that we might have to drive in bad weather or that we might use it as an excuse to put off coming. It's only raining here." Gaby's sisters lived about three hours south.

"There is real snow but it was warmer earlier so it's not sticking. I think it'd have to come down for a long time before it causes any problems for you."

"That's good. Though I really don't think it would be a big deal if we ended up leaving a few hours late."

"You know Mom doesn't like to change her plans."

"Well, it doesn't sound necessary anyway so I think we'll all survive."

"Okay," Gaby said, "I'll see you soon."

She put her phone down to get ready for bed and she let her thoughts go back to Owen. Gaby wasn't disappointed with how the night had ended. She didn't care that he hadn't actually kissed her because she was satisfied to see that he might be thinking about it. There was no need to rush the change and she might have been too nervous to enjoy it anyway.

She guessed he'd stopped because he had mistaken her nervousness for uncertainty. But what if he hadn't kissed her because *he* was the one who wasn't sure? If she could manage to stay calm next time everything would be fine as soon as he was ready. Maybe. As long as they weren't awkward about the near miss. She admitted to herself that that was a significant caveat. And being calm suddenly sounded challenging as well. The nervous energy made her run a few laps around her apartment as she felt some of her Christmas excitement refocusing on her birthday. Something told her this year's would be memorable.

Chapter 13

Owen drove to the city in the morning. There were no tree lots in Hartford. He found a tree that was about four feet tall. It was fairly narrow but with full branches. It fit in the trunk of his car with the tree stand he'd bought first. He was a little worried that Gaby might look out the window and see the tree before he got it set up and more worried that it would take longer to set up than he expected.

He noticed on his way up the stairs that Gaby had added some silver garland to her front door. That was already there when he left, wasn't it? Did she get up in the middle of the night to decorate? He would not put that past her. He shook his head and hurried into his apartment with the tree. It was as much of a pain to make it stand straight up as he thought it would be but he did get it done.

At exactly 10 am, Gaby texted: Are you ready for me?

He replied with a simple yes and waited for her knock. She came in wearing her own coat and carrying his. "Thanks for this," she said as she handed it back and dropped a small bag by the door. "I brought everything with me so I can go straight to my parents' house from here." She took off her gray coat and dropped it over the back of the couch. The sleeve dropped onto the head of Christmas Pig, who was still smiling merrily.

Owen stood holding his own jacket and waiting for Gaby to notice the tree in the corner of the room.

She looked at him expectantly and with a hint of anxiety.

Had she noticed how close he'd come to kissing her? And did she feel good or bad anxiety about that? Why couldn't she give him a clue? Owen looked at the tree and then back at her.

She turned the same way and then grinned broadly. "You got a tree! Is that a real tree!?" She walked over to it and inhaled deeply. "It smells so nice. But it's naked." Owen had followed her to the tree and she turned to him hopefully. "Tell me you plan to decorate it."

"I plan to let you do it. That's the present."

"Yea!" Gaby put her arms up in celebration. "Where are the ornaments? Do you have lights? Can anyone see it through this window? Where did you get the ornaments? Have you been hiding them?"

Gaby was looking around the room as she talked and Owen loved to see her enthusiasm. This had so far been a good idea. "Hang on a second," he said. He took his coat into his bedroom and came out carrying a cardboard box. There was a small wrapped gift and a plastic shopping bag on top of it. "I got white lights so they match the ones outside. Is that okay?"

"Sure. I like white ones, too. Though actually I picked those out so maybe you wouldn't know it was me."

Owen smiled at her. "Did you really think, even for a second, that I would suspect anyone else of Christmas-bombing my porch?"

"Maybe for a second."

He put the box down next to Gaby and handed her the gift. "I just borrowed a box of ornaments from my mom but this... I thought you should have something to open."

Gaby took the box and simply held it. She looked happy but there was something else he couldn't read. "Did you, um, forget how to open presents?" he asked.

A faint smile appeared before she pressed her lips together to squash it. Then she tore the paper off and opened the box. There was a pair of glass spheres inside. One was full of green glitter and hung from a red ribbon. The other had red glitter and a green ribbon.

"Look at that," Owen said, "I actually found glitter that is contained."

"Wow, I love these." Gaby held one up by the ribbon and watched it spin in front of her. It didn't sound as though she was just being nice. "I hope I don't drop it though."

"I didn't think of that," Owen said. "Let's get them safely on the tree."

Gaby put the new ornament back in the box and cocked her head to the side. "You really haven't done this in a while, have you?"

"What do you mean?"

"The lights go on first."

"Okay. Maybe I should just get out of the way."

"Don't worry," Gaby said with a smile. "I'll let you know if you're doing anything wrong."

Owen hoped it wouldn't come to that. He'd had second and third and fourth thoughts about this idea even before last night. There was likely no backing out now though. It was already in the box.

Gaby opened the lights and went to work like the expert she was. It didn't take her more than five minutes to get the lights wrapped around the evergreen. "Amazing," she said as she stepped back to admire the newly glowing corner of the room. "You got exactly the right amount of lights without even knowing what you're doing." She pointed at the box Owen had brought out. "These are the ornaments?"

"Yeah, my mom has about a zillion so she doesn't use them all. I didn't go through the box at all. I just peeked to make sure it looked like ornaments. You don't have to use anything you don't like."

Gaby reached for the lid and then stood up again. "I almost forgot to put the new ones on first." She grabbed the small box and pulled out the red and green ornaments she'd unwrapped. She dangled the green one from her finger and held it out to Owen. "You find a place for this one."

He put his hand under the glass. "Are you sure you trust me with this?"

"Of course."

"I'm not sure *I* trust me not to drop it."

The glass touched his hand as Gaby lowered it. It might have been his imagination but it felt as though she spent more time than necessary working her finger out of the ribbon while her hand skimmed his. Then she smiled and turned to hang the red ornament. When she stepped back to let him get to the tree, he noticed that her cheeks were pink. That was not his imagination. But was she just excited about the decorating or was she embarrassed about having made an excuse to touch him? Was she flirting?

Owen hung up the ornament she'd handed him while Gaby opened the box. "Ooh... silver bells." She pulled out a flat container with a dozen silver bell-shaped decorations, each with a dark green bow on top. She hummed the song "Silver Bells" as she worked and gently rang each bell before finding it a place on the tree.

Next she found something wrapped in tissue paper that turned out to be a musical ceramic Santa. "This doesn't go on a tree," she said.

"I told you these are my mom's. I'm hoping it isn't all her rejects. Anything that won't work you can just leave in the box."

Gaby turned the Santa over and wound it up. It played "White Christmas." She said, "We don't have to stick to the tree, right? A decoration is a decoration. Because it's my birthday?" She turned questioning eyes on him.

He was counting on that attitude. Owen wasn't lying about not going through the box but he had slipped a few random items from his mom's closet in with the ornaments to make his own addition less suspicious. He tried to appear mildly reluctant as he nodded. "Yeah, go ahead."

She let the Santa continue his song on an end table and came back to the box. She found a bag of beaded ornaments for the tree next and a long string of gingerbread men that she carefully spiraled around it. Then she pulled out something that made her eyebrows knit together. "What is this?" she said as she held up a green blob that appeared to be made out of hard plastic.

Owen didn't know what it was at first either. Then he noticed two small holes in the top and they nudged a memory. "Oh, I think there's another piece for that." He knelt by the box and dug out a Santa. "This one's for salt," he said, "and the green thing is for pepper. It fits together like this." He took the part from Gaby as he spoke and put it on the Santa's shoulder so that it resembled a bag of toys. Then he moved to put them both back in the box.

"A decoration is a decoration," Gaby said again. "Can't we put him on the kitchen counter? You don't have to fill it."

Owen shrugged and took the Santa into the kitchen. Gaby was already hanging more ornaments when he returned. She picked up a flat box with a clear plastic lid. It contained six red glass balls with Christmas trees of silver glitter on the sides. She removed the lid and offered the box to Owen. "Do you want to hang one of these?"

"I'll get glitter all over my hands."

"They're so pretty and you're not helping. You don't feel left out?"

He shook his head but pulled an ornament from the box. "I'll hang one if you want me to. But this is supposed to be your present." He reached over and hooked the ball on a branch. "You are having fun, right?"

Her smile was brighter than a whole string of Christmas lights. "This is an awesome birthday present! Thank you. Did I say thank you yet? I can't believe you're finally letting me get your place decked out properly. Though I'm going to miss calling you Scrooge."

"There's always next year."

"No way. You've crossed over now. There's no going back." Gaby had hung all the other red balls while she was talking and was looking into the box. There were only a few items left and Owen knew she could see the mistletoe now. What would she do with it? He watched as she pushed a few things around, seemingly indecisive about which item to pick up next. She grabbed a few random ornaments and hung them quickly before her hand closed on the mistletoe. "This isn't for the tree either," she said.

"Yeah, that can stay in the box."

"I think I heard someone say that a decoration is a decoration. But don't worry I'll…" She trailed off with a tiny smile as she looked around the room. "I'll put it in the corner of the kitchen. There we can see it but not be surprised by it or anything. Do you have tape?"

Owen went with her into the kitchen and opened a drawer. He handed her a roll of masking tape. She put a piece on the string attached to the mistletoe and dragged a chair over to the far corner. Even standing on the chair, however, she was not quite tall enough to reach the ceiling. She gave a small hop to try to make the tape stick and she missed.

"Gaby, let me help." Owen walked closer. "You're going to fall off that chair if you—"

She jumped again before he could finish the sentence and the tape grabbed the ceiling on her second try. She looked down at Owen and her eyes were wide. "Look what you just did."

"Uh…" Owen took a big step backward. He hadn't meant to

corner her. The whole point was to see if she would come to him. "I don't think it counts if you're still hanging it up."

Gaby climbed off the chair. "Do you really think I can let you ignore a Christmas tradition? Come on." She offered her cheek with a tap of her finger. "A quick peck with cover it."

It was clear she was trying to act more nonchalant than she felt. Owen thought it best to oblige before the air around them got any thicker. He stepped closer again, watching Gaby for signs that she was going to change her mind. He stopped before he touched her cheek though. He was too close.

The temptation to find out if she'd turn away from a real kiss was too strong. He found her lips slowly, giving her time to stop him. She did not. He kissed her softly and lingered, trying to delay the moment she asked him what he thought he was doing. When he opened his eyes, he saw that she had tears in hers.

"Gaby?" His voice sounded unnatural, strangled.

"I gotta go," she said as she ducked around him. She grabbed her coat and her bag and left so fast the door stayed open behind her.

Owen could hear her running down the stairs outside. She was crying. He made her cry? He sat on the floor in the kitchen, right next to the chair Gaby had used. Of all the times he'd imagined kissing her and all the different outcomes, crying had never entered the picture. Why didn't she just move if she didn't want him to kiss her?

The tape gave up and dropped the sprig of mistletoe onto the floor nearby with a faint though wretched clunk.

Chapter 14

Gaby jumped into her car and started driving. Her parents would be happy if she was early. She drove to the park instead and stopped her car where she had a good view of the town Christmas tree. She stared hard at the tree because her eyelids seemed to have been painted with a picture of Owen's stricken face and she couldn't allow her eyes to close and show her what he looked like when he saw her tears.

The ornaments on the tree were large and red. She tried to focus on a particular red star. Most of the snow from the previous night had melted but there was a tiny patch in the tree's shadow.

The minutes ticked by surprisingly quickly while she tried not to think about anything, especially not about how badly she had screwed things up with Owen. She put her hands on her face and still kept her eyes open, studying the lines on her palms and feeling the heat that still hadn't faded. She tried to concentrate on Jess and Hannah. She would be happy to see her sisters again. And she needed to go. She needed to get there on time because if she was late, her mom would call Owen to find out what was taking so long.

She drove to her parents' house and let them welcome her with birthday hugs. The three of them sat together and she said very little while she listened to them chatter about having the whole family back together again.

Jess and Hannah arrived a short time later, just as planned. Hannah had the same dark curls as Gaby, though hers were currently longer. Jess had inherited very straight, lighter brown hair from their mom. There was a great deal of hugging amidst a chorus of "Welcome home," and "Happy birthday." The younger girls put their suitcases upstairs with help from their dad and then returned to be grilled about their exams and what grades they'd received.

Gaby pretended to listen. Until someone caught her pretending.

"Gaby?"

She looked up to see that Jess was eyeing her strangely. "What?" Gaby said.

"I asked if you have to work on Monday."

"Oh. No, I have the whole week off."

"Good," said Hannah. "You'll come with us then?"

"Come where?"

Jess and Hannah exchanged amused glances before Hannah said, "We were just talking about going to the city to finish our Christmas shopping. You'll come?"

"Yeah, okay. I guess that means you already got something for me?"

Hannah smiled coyly. "I'm sure we can figure something out."

"That sounds like a no," Gaby said. She wasn't worried though. They had shopped for each other together in the past and managed not to spoil any surprises. The only person Gaby had left to shop for though was Owen. What if she couldn't get him anything now? What if they couldn't get past the awkward mess she'd just made? And why did everything remind her of what she was trying not to think about?

"Gaby?"

She looked up to see that her mom was talking to her. Everyone else had gotten up to move to the dining room for lunch.

"I'm coming."

"Is something wrong?" her mom asked.

"No. Sorry I got distracted."

Penny Bryant gave her daughter a concerned look as they followed the others to the next room. "Are you distracted by anything specific?"

"Nothing for you to worry about."

Her mom didn't press but she didn't appear less concerned either. She'd made some very rich mac and cheese for lunch and it was one of Gaby's favorites. She only had a few bites before she mostly pushed it around her plate. At some point Hannah stood up and said, "Okay, it's time to get to the bottom of this." She motioned Jess to come, too, and they each grabbed one of Gaby's arms.

Jess looked at their parents as they marched Gaby from the room. "We're going to make Gaby talk to us and then we'll be back for dessert."

126

Gaby reluctantly let her sisters drag her to one of the upstairs bedrooms. It was the one the younger girls had shared when they were kids. There was a pair of twin beds. One had a light purple flowery comforter and the other had dark purple stripes. Hannah lightly pushed Gaby onto the striped bed before she and Jess sat opposite her on the flowers.

"Okay," Jess said, "spill it."

"What?" Gaby asked.

"Come on." Hannah gave an exaggerated eye roll. "You have guy problem written all over you. Just tell us what's going on already."

Gaby wondered if there was any chance they'd make her feel better or if they'd just laugh.

"Mom told us there's been some rumors floating around about you and that guy at the bank," Jess said. "What really happened with you two?"

"Nothing," Gaby said. "We went out once and there was no spark. We're friendly now. That's really it."

"So this is not about him?"

"No."

"It's Owen then, right?"

Gaby gave the most noncommittal shrug possible as a response.

"I knew it," Hannah said. "You've finally fallen for him and don't know how to tell him."

"Not exactly."

Her sisters looked at each other excitedly and Jess said, "It's about time."

Hannah turned back to Gaby. "Just tell us what happened."

"All right." Even if they laughed, Gaby couldn't keep the weight of it inside any longer. "I went over there this morning for a birthday present. He got a tree and let me decorate it."

Simultaneous "awws" came from her sisters.

"I know," Gaby said. "It was great. He borrowed a box of decorations from his mom and everything. It was fun. And then…"

"Yes?" Hannah prompted.

"Then what?"

"I found some… mistletoe… in the box."

"Oh, boy!" Hannah's eyes widened and Jess scooted a bit closer to the edge of the bed.

"I wanted to hang it up because... I don't know really. I guess I thought that might... um..."

"Oh, no," Jess said. "You wanted him to kiss you and he didn't? That is bad."

"That *is* bad," Hannah agreed. "I thought for sure he was just waiting for you to come around."

Gaby sighed. "That's not what happened."

"Okay." Hannah looked at Jess for a moment. "We won't interrupt again. Did you hang up the mistletoe?"

"I did. I put it up in a corner where I thought we couldn't get under it by accident. But I couldn't reach and he tried to help and well..."

"So you ended up together under it?" Hannah asked. "Did he do that on purpose?"

"I don't think so. He tried to back away and I'm the one who insisted. I thought we could do an innocent kiss on the cheek and not be awkward. But," Gaby felt her face reach about the temperature of lava, "he... he really kissed me."

"Really!?"

"That's great," Jess said.

Both of her sisters looked very happy and very confused. Gaby shook her head. She buried her face in her hands and mumbled something her sisters couldn't understand.

"What?" they asked together.

Gaby tried to push the red from her face with her fingers before she looked up. Very quietly she said, "I cried."

"You what?" Hannah looked at a complete loss for understanding.

Jess looked as though she was trying not to laugh.

"I couldn't help it," Gaby said. "He sort of caught me off guard and I got all emotional and... he looked so freaked out when he noticed that I was crying and I was so embarrassed I... I left."

"You left without saying anything?"

"I couldn't help that either. I just had an instinct to run. It was too strong to ignore."

Jess had her lips pressed together as though she might burst any second but she was trying to keep herself from laughing out loud.

Hannah still looked as though she was struggling to make sense of the situation. "So he kissed you and then you left crying? Poor Owen."

"Oh, I know," Gaby moaned. "I need to talk to him. He probably thinks... I guess I don't know what he thinks but it can't be anything good."

"Why don't you call him now?" Jess said. Thinking about Owen's reaction seemed to have sobered her up.

"I can't. I should talk to him in person but not yet. I'm still embarrassed and confused and I don't have any idea what to say."

"How about, 'I'm sorry I ran away. Kiss me again so we can get it right.'" Jess was still enjoying the situation somewhat.

Gaby twisted her hands together in her lap. "This thing is... What if... What if he only kissed me to give me a hard time about insisting on the tradition? What if he doesn't... I mean, we've been friends a long time. He might not want to change that."

"You know there's no way he'd mess with you."

"No way," Hannah agreed. "There had to have been some strong feelings on his side. I don't think you'd have gotten all choked up by a kiss that didn't mean anything."

"Ugh." Gaby covered her face again. "I don't believe this happened. He almost kissed me last night, too."

"Wait, wait," Jess said. "What does almost mean?"

Hannah looked indignant. "What other juicy details are you leaving out?"

Gaby sat back and pulled her feet onto the bed so she could hug her knees. "Right as I was leaving yesterday... there was a moment."

"I like moments," Hannah said with a grin. "Describe it."

"I can't," Gaby said. "He just looked at me and I somehow knew he was thinking about kissing me but he didn't. So I went over there this morning afraid it might be awkward or something but he was all normal and friendly and I thought he wanted to pretend it didn't happen. I tried to go along with that because maybe he was still sorting out some feelings or I don't know." She stopped and buried her face in her knees. "I just don't know what to say to him. I made it *so* much more awkward."

"Don't worry," Hannah said. "Just make sure when you talk that you use the words 'happy tears.' Let him know you're not upset about it and you guys will be tighter than ever in no time." She stood up. "Come on. If we don't get back downstairs soon, Mom will come up and listen at the door."

"All right." Gaby rubbed her hands over her face as she stood in a fruitless attempt to make herself look normal. She probably only succeeded in adding white splotches to the red.

Their parents had the table cleared by the time they returned and the whole family sat in the living room sharing a plate of cookies. Gaby was still a little quieter than usual, but she managed to keep up with the conversation enough to avoid any probing questions. Her dad pulled out some old board games after dinner and birthday cake and it was fairly late by the time Gaby made it back to her apartment.

She'd had her phone off all day because she didn't know if she was more afraid of hearing from Owen or not hearing from him. She stared at the phone while she changed into pajamas and while she brushed her teeth. It was daring her to pick it up. Her fingers trembled as she checked for messages from Owen. He'd sent one simple text: I'm sorry. Please call me.

She held her phone tightly. She knew she needed to respond, knew she was the one who needed to apologize. Finally she sent: I'm sorry too. Can we talk after church tomorrow?

Owen immediately replied with: OK

She put the phone down and gently ran her hand over the wall. It was difficult to think that he was on the other side of it waiting for her to explain. She felt guilty for putting it off. Her fear won out over the guilt as she climbed into bed.

Sleep was elusive. Gaby managed a few restless hours of it though and felt better when she woke up. The embarrassment had faded and left a bit of hope. Regardless of what happened afterwards, Owen had kissed her. He'd apparently *wanted* to kiss her. Maybe they could get past the tension to something better.

She drove herself to church rather than ride with her family, but she sought them out in their typical pew. She spotted Owen in his usual place and he was smiling at someone greeting him but she could see the way he forced it. He was miserable and it was her fault. She smiled and waved when she caught his eye, trying to convey the coming apology. He waved back uncertainly.

The two families approached each other after mass for small

talk. Owen's parents welcomed Gaby's sisters home and Gaby's parents wished Owen's family a safe trip out of town. Gaby found a moment to discretely ask Owen if he'd meet her at her apartment.

"Are you going straight home?" he asked.

She nodded. "I'm supposed to have lunch with the family, but they can start without me."

"Okay. We'll talk." He appeared to be looking forward to the talk about as much as a prison sentence.

Jess nudged Gaby on the way to the parking lot. "See," she said. "It's going to be fine."

"Because we can be polite to each other?"

"No. Because he wants to talk about it. He wants it to be okay, too."

Gaby turned to watch Owen across the lot. He was looking at her while he got into his car. She wanted things to be more than okay between them. It felt weird to be going home when they could be talking right away but Gaby was certain that this was a conversation she wanted to have in private. The drive home seemed faster than usual because she wanted it to be slower. She was still trying to put together some words. Why was "I'm sorry" the only way to apologize? She'd never meant it like this before.

Owen was sitting on the steps between their apartments when she got there. "Hi," he said.

"Hi."

He pointed up as she unlocked her door. "When did you do this?"

"The garland?"

"Yeah." He stepped inside after her.

Gaby closed the door and Owen stood in front of it. He was probably trying to make sure she couldn't run away again. That wasn't a bad idea. "I, um, you didn't put that there?" she asked.

"No. You thought I put garland on your door?"

"Well, I didn't."

Owen was quiet for a moment before he said, "Maybe it's an apology from your vandal."

"That would be... nice. I guess."

"Yeah." Owen was still blocking the door instead of coming in and making himself at home like he normally would. She wondered if maybe he was the one preparing to bolt.

Gaby braced herself and dove in. "Look, Owen, I'm sorry about yesterday."

"*You're* sorry?"

"Yes. I shouldn't have run away and I'm sorry about that."

Owen put his hand through his hair and turned away. "But I upset you and..." He didn't seem to know what else he wanted to say.

"You didn't. I wasn't upset at all I was... overwhelmed."

"Overwhelmed," Owen repeated slowly. "Is that... is that better than upset?"

"Maybe."

"Maybe?" Owen appeared bewildered by her answer.

"It depends on... it depends what you were going for."

"I definitely wasn't *trying* to overwhelm you."

"Okay, here goes..." Gaby sucked in a big, nervous breath. "Did you kiss me because I was being ridiculous about the mistletoe or because... because..." Owen seemed to be waiting for the other choice and Gaby couldn't figure out how to put it into the right words... or any words. She switched course and said, "How would you feel if I said those were happy tears?"

Owen blinked at her a few times and she had no idea what he was thinking. "But why would you run?"

"Because I was embarrassed." Gaby covered part of her face with her hand. She was still embarrassed. "I didn't know if you were kidding around or what and I was all... mushy."

He gently pushed her hand away from her face and put his fingers under her chin to encourage her to look at him. There was no more misery in his eyes. Only a hopeful disbelief swam in the blue. "Happy tears?"

She nodded slowly, forcing a smile that she hoped would keep her surging emotions dry this time.

"So I could tell you?"

Anticipation swelled up in Gaby and made her head feel light.

"I could tell you I love you," Owen said, "and I don't have to pretend I mean like a friend? And I don't have to say I love you for your cookies? I can just tell you and you're okay with that?"

"I'm okay with that."

"Gaby, I think you're telling *me* something very important here." He moved closer and the hand on her chin slipped around to the back of her neck where his fingers plunged into her hair.

"What I am telling you?"

"That I don't need mistletoe."

Gaby let out a nervous laugh. It was weird to have Owen so close, good weird but still weird. She shook her head slightly.

He leaned in a bit and asked, "Are you sure?"

She was sure. But she didn't say that. She answered by kissing him. He responded with none of the hesitation of the first kiss and no trace of kidding around. Instead of tears, Gaby felt giddy smiles leaking from her face. "So," she said, "I think this was a good talk. How about you?"

Owen nodded. He still had his hand in her hair, twisting the curls around his fingers.

"I don't want to leave, but I know my mom and they're not really starting without me. They're sitting around talking about what's taking me so long."

"Yeah." Owen winced. "I didn't actually tell my parents that I wasn't going straight to their house."

"You didn't?" It wasn't funny but Gaby was laughing anyway.

"If I told them I was coming to see you first, they'd want to know why."

"I see. Thank you for not telling them, by the way. It sounds like we both need to go though." She didn't move and neither did Owen. She said, "Will you come back and see me later?"

"What time?"

"With Jess and Hannah in town I should probably stay for dinner. Maybe sevenish?"

"Just let me know when you get home," Owen said as he moved his hand from her shoulder all the way down her arm before he took her hand. "Let's go."

Chapter 15

Owen walked to his parents' house feeling very light. They let him get away with a vague excuse only because they could tell he was happier than before the delay. They gave him a few presents, mostly clothes, after lunch since they were leaving the following morning.

Owen and Jimmy had agreed sometime in high school that they would not exchange gifts. Jimmy reminded his brother of that agreement as they stopped on the porch for their usual chat. "Thanks again," he said, "for the gift of one less thing to shop for."

"Same to you."

"What did you get for Ava?"

"I bought some baby stuff and called it a gift for the whole family. What did you get her?"

"Nothing yet," Jimmy said. "I'm hoping if I mention it on the drive down, Mom will pick something out for me."

"That's cheating."

Jimmy shrugged. "And buying one present for three people is not? If I can get Mom to wrap it for me, I'll do that, too."

"You sure you can survive that many hours in a car with Mom and Dad?"

"No problem. I'm bringing headphones."

"So, um, how's that brilliant plan of yours working out?"

"All of my plans are brilliant," Jimmy said with a smile. "Which one are you referring to?"

"The one where Summer fixes you up with Emma."

"Oh. It's going surprisingly well as a matter of fact. Summer thinks I'm thinking about it."

Owen laughed. "Giving it a lot of serious thought, are you?"

Jimmy put his hands up defensively. "Honestly, I'd have just agreed but Summer didn't give me a chance. She was like, 'I have this idea but you're not allowed to say anything right now. You have to think about it.' So I told her I'd think about it."

Owen shook his head slightly and checked his watch. Still at least four hours until he could see Gaby again.

"So," Jimmy said, "it doesn't take a genius to figure out that Gaby had something to do with you being late for lunch and you're no longer in a huge funk. Are you just glad to be back at square one or…" Jimmy lifted his eyebrows in expectation of Owen filling in the blank.

"I'm not sure what exactly constitutes square two but… maybe."

"Congratulations! But don't say anything else. If I know something, Mom will sense it and be relentless on the drive."

Owen wasn't about to give details anyway. He slapped his brother on the back. "Well, I'll see you after Christmas."

Jimmy returned the gesture. It was about as close as they ever came to hugging. "Later, man." Jimmy was headed to work and Owen returned home to wait for Gaby. He liked the general direction they were headed but something still felt unresolved.

****

Gaby's parents didn't ask her what was happening with Owen. This was partly out of respect for her privacy and partly because they didn't have to ask. Her sisters painted a fairly clear picture with their hints. Jess made several comments about Owen giving Gaby an early Christmas present. Hannah made a few references to mistletoe. Each comment was followed by silly smiles aimed at Gaby. Between the teasing and the fact that she was going shopping with them the next day, Gaby didn't feel guilty about leaving her sisters right after dinner.

She walked up the stairs and unlocked her apartment door. Then she tiptoed over to Owen's side. She knocked on his door before rushing back to her own side. The sound of Owen opening and closing his door made her smile. A minute later she got a text from him that said: Welcome home. I'll be over in ten minutes.

Gaby pulled out some yarn to amuse herself for those ten minutes. She carried it to the door when Owen arrived. He was holding the musical Santa.

"What is that?" she asked, ignoring the nervous flutter in her stomach.

Owen pretended to cover the tiny statue's ears. "He thought you were his biggest fan and you don't even know who he is?"

"Santa is wonderful. But why is he here?"

"I thought you were supposed to bring Christmas stuff to your neighbors once your place was overflowing with it."

"Overflowing?" Gaby scoffed. "You still only have the bare minimum of holiday spirit over there. But there's room for Santa on that table." She nodded towards a small round bistro table in the corner. It was white with red and green dots on the legs and a Christmas tree on its surface. Gaby had found it at a yard sale two years earlier and painted it for Christmas.

Owen found a place for the Santa next to a pair of red candles in wreath-shaped holders and a mini crèche. "Okay," he said as he turned around, "let me ask you the same question."

Gaby tried to ask what he meant with a confused expression.

He looked at the mess of yarn she was holding. "What is that?"

"Oh. Finger weaving." She glanced self-consciously at the ball of red yarn in her right hand. It was wrapped around the fingers of her left hand with a twisted tail of it hanging down to drag slightly on the floor.

Owen did not look as though his question had been answered.

"It's something we used to do when we were kids. Don't you remember? Jess was reminding me of it today, saying how she was so impressed when I showed her how. I think I was about nine or ten so I guess I had a lot more dexterity than a five-year-old."

"Now that you mention it, I guess I do remember people – girls – wearing yarn necklaces and stuff in elementary school. Never saw the work in progress though."

"Well, you're welcome for the riveting behind the scenes peek. I was just messing around, trying to see if I remembered, and then I thought that if I made it long enough I could wrap it around my tree."

"Because you can still see some of the tree sticking out from all the other ornaments?"

"Stop it," Gaby said. "My tree is beautiful."

She turned to admire the tree and heard Owen say, "Like you." His voice was low and quiet, so quiet she wasn't sure if she was supposed to hear it. She didn't understand the odd tension in the air. Everything had seemed fine – great actually, really really great – when they parted earlier in the day. Admitting that she enjoyed his kiss so much it brought tears to her eyes would have been humiliating if he hadn't immediately said he loved her. Now they were supposed to be on the same page, not standing stiffly as though their relationship was uncertain.

"Gaby?" Owen said.

She turned to face him.

"Are you okay?"

"Is this weird for you?" she asked.

"Your finger weaving? Very."

"No." She looked down at her hands. It *was* ridiculous but if she put it down she'd have to start over. "I meant that... I don't know, we had sort of a big talk and yet things don't feel all that different."

Owen grinned. "You expected me to come over spouting poetry instead of teasing you about twisting yarn all over your hands?"

"Of course not."

He wiggled his eyebrows suggestively. "You just need more time to get used to having passionate daydreams about me?"

Gaby let out a short burst of laughter.

"That's funny, huh?"

"It is a little funny," she said. It was funny when he said it. It wasn't funny when it happened. She wasn't about to tell him that.

"You're not..." Owen took a few steps closer and looked more serious. "Are you still overwhelmed?"

"Maybe."

"I didn't surprise you, did I? I mean, I kind of thought... I thought we were headed this way."

"Yeah. I just didn't know how we were going to bring it up. I guess it was good that we lucked into mistletoe because it made us talk."

A guilty smile slipped onto Owen's face. "Um, this might be where I need to confess something."

"Wait a minute." Gaby reached both hands behind him and passed her ball of yarn from one hand to the other and back. Now she still had the ball of yarn in one hand and a mess of it in the other. In between, it was wrapped twice around Owen's waist.

"What are you doing?" he asked.

"Getting some answers. Now... did you know there was mistletoe in the box?"

"Yes."

"Did you want me to find it?"

"Yes."

Gaby eyed him suspiciously. "Did you join me under it on purpose?"

"No."

"No?"

Owen gently tugged one of her curls. "Hey," he said, "with your hands tied up you can't stop me from playing with your hair."

She shook her head without really trying to stop him. "Just answer the question."

"I did."

"You said no."

"That's my answer."

"Okay," Gaby said, "what exactly was your plan?"

"I was just hoping for clues. I think you could tell I almost kissed you on Friday but I couldn't tell... I didn't know if you wanted me to. If you had left the mistletoe in the box, that would have been a clear hint that you didn't want to give me an opening."

"You want to know what I thought when I saw it?"

"Yes, I would," Owen said with a prompt nod.

"I wondered if there was any way to get us both under it without being obvious."

"What's wrong with obvious?" He put his hands on her shoulders as though he wanted to shake her, but kept the touch tender. "You could have told me."

"I didn't know that at the time. I suspected, but I wanted to *know* if you wanted more."

"Gaby," he let his hands slide down to hold each of hers, yarn and all, "I never wanted less. Now tell me what I need to do to get out of your little trap."

"That," she said, "should be obvious."

Owen didn't wait for more hints. He kissed her, first on her mouth and then on the side of her neck. He pressed his lips to her skin a few more times as he worked his way up to her ear where he whispered, "I really think you need to let me back up now."

She dropped the yarn and nodded.

He untwisted himself and placed the red mass back in her hand. "Thanks," she said.

"So do you want to watch TV or something while you finish that?" He nodded towards her hands.

"In a minute. I just figured out why things feel unsettled. I didn't tell you I... I love you, too."

Owen smiled at her. "That does sort of put a bow on things."

"A Christmas analogy! Now I love you more."

~~ The End ~~

Thanks for reading *The Christmas Project*.

More *Stories From Hartford*

Andrew's Key (January 2014)

Talk around Hartford is that the old Hilson house is haunted. Its new owner, Rebecca Hilson, doesn't believe that. She's more concerned with the decades of junk that has accumulated and for which she is now responsible. She doesn't know what to do with any of it or even how to approach sorting through it all.

Her new neighbor, Andrew Lately, is happy to offer some words of wisdom and the help of his grandson, Charlie, to get her started. Charlie makes it clear right away that he is interested in more than helping Rebecca move boxes. She doesn't know if she can return those feelings. In fact, recent events have made her question her ability to feel much of anything.

Will Charlie's patience pay off or will it take a real ghost to help Rebecca understand the nature of love?

Jealousy & Yams (April 2014)

Luke Foster has been accused of being too nice for his own good. He enjoys being helpful though and never thought it was a problem until he met Summer. Now he believes she feels indebted to him and it isn't gratitude he wants from her.

Summer Slough feels guilty for using Luke. She also feels an attraction to him that she doesn't know how to handle. It's beginning to look as though her mistakes and inexperience will keep them apart.

Lucky for both of them, Hartford's annual Yam Fest is right around the corner. The community event has a way of bringing people together... maybe even Summer and Luke.

Collecting Zebras (August 2014)

Angel Melling is determined to find a husband. The long held goal has recently morphed into an obsession. Being the new girl in a small town does have some advantages though. Angel quickly catches the eye of several of Hartford's eligible bachelors.

Her quest for a husband appears to be on the right track as she embarks on the most active dating of her life. But as the guys are ruled out one after another, Angel begins to fear that she'll run out of options. Will Angel find a guy who meets all the criteria for her happily ever after?

www.ingramcontent.com/pod-product-compliance
Lightning Source LLC
Chambersburg PA
CBHW030534130626
46552CB00006B/2245